Y0-EGF-510

Also by Mary Beth Craft

Where Do I Put My Purse While I Preach? — cartoons

*Would Somebody Hold My Purse
While I Preach?* — cartoons

Many Happy Returns — a New Orleans vignette

Goldengrove

Goldengrove

Mary Beth Craft

PEN & INK

PEN & INK is an imprint of
Genesis Press, Inc.
315 Third Avenue North
Columbus, Mississippi 39701

Goldengrove

ISBN 1-885478-97-6

Printed in the United States of America

FIRST EDITION

Original Cover Photo
©Corbis Images 1999

For my kind and caring family
With special thanks to Susan

And also for Barney, my good luck charm

Goldengrove

Chapter One

"Anne," my brother David had said, "the ghosts don't sing on Wednesday nights." The telephone connection was bad and I didn't answer at once. "Remember that, Anne." There was urgency in his voice. "The ghosts don't sing on Wednesday night because—" and the line went dead.

That was three days ago and now as I drove across Lake Pontchartrain through the early morning October haze, I tried to sort out things David had written me and to connect them with that last brief phone call.

I knew he was still in north Mississippi where he had gone to investigate the legend that one of the area's antebellum homes was actively haunted (he was working on a Ph.D. dissertation in psychic research) because the call had been collect, and I distinctly heard the operator say, "I have a collect call for anyone from David Whitehead in Blue Valley, Mississippi. Will you accept the call?"

David had been in Blue Valley a month and I had received word from him each week, so far two telephone calls and two letters. The Whiteheads had shrunk to the two of us and our dog, Bottom, a big shaggy black dog with a few white spots, and the three of us lived together in our huge old family home in the Garden District of New Orleans. That house itself seemed haunted, especially on rainy winter nights when its moans and groans competed with the whining winds outside. I think our home was the source of David's interest in ghosts and such.

David's strange call had come late on a Saturday night, and I tried Sunday to call him back, but the motel manager informed me he had checked out about eleven Saturday morning saying he would be staying with a friend. Since David had mentioned very few names in connection with his research, I had almost nothing to go on. I finally decided I was overly upset, but Monday at noon when I went home to check on Bottom, I found a postcard from David mailed Saturday. (This was 1970, when the post office gave fast, efficient service even between backwoods Mississippi and New Orleans.) The card read: "There is not much I can tell you, but I'm sure you will understand how really hard I'm working—all night last night and Wednesday night too, like those wonderful old summer nights long ago. I am afraid—" No signature. Not even "Dear Anne" at the beginning. The card had been folded in half somewhere along the way, then smoothed out, and knowing my brother's neat nature, I found the card as strange as the telephone call. I spent the afternoon arranging my editing job to be away the rest of the week, and that evening I packed my car so Bottom and I could leave early the next morning for Blue Valley to try to find out what was going on. I was to wish later that I had told several people, including the police, where I was going.

The chilly haze lifted about nine o'clock as we were rolling along the pine-covered hills of south Mississippi. I pulled into a rest area to take down the top of my red Fiat so Bottom and I could feel the soft October sun on our heads—his black and white one and my blonde one. Bottom leaped out and sniffed around the nearby trees and then bounced back in, carefully folding his large body into the back seat of the little car.

Before driving on, I pulled David's two letters out of my purse and reread them.

The first letter was written three days after David arrived in Blue Valley. In it he told me the name of the motel where he was staying and gave a glowing description of the house he had gone to study. "Goldengrove may or may not be haunted," he wrote, "but haunted or not it is without a doubt the most fascinating house I have ever seen, even more exciting than the haunted houses in New Orleans." In spite of my worry, I had to smile at the thought of David's obsessive idea that ghosts do exist, an idea so at odds with his personality and looks: an outgoing happy-go-lucky young man of great intelligence with the same brown eyes and soft blond curls I saw in my own mirror.

Enclosed in the envelope with that first letter was a photocopy of an article from a Memphis morning newspaper, dated a year before, that described an accident at Goldengrove which took the life of the young woman whose husband, Rockford Collins Andrews, had inherited Goldengrove some five years back and who had devoted her time and energies to helping her husband restore the run-down reputedly haunted house to its original glory. On the day of her death, she had been occupied with something on the third floor balcony overlooking the open space that went from first floor on past third to a skylight beyond and had lost her balance, falling to the marble floor below. Professor Andrews of the nearby university English department had been the first to reach his wife's side. The article stated that he was reluctant to discuss the matter, but the cook and a maid both told interviewers that they heard Mrs. Andrews say something just before she died: "The ghosts were singing a sad song last night."

David's second letter, written during his second week in Blue Valley, was a very brief note to the effect that all was going well and that he hoped to go inside Goldengrove that night to try to hear the singing ghosts firsthand.

The heavy early morning traffic had thinned down to fewer eighteen-wheelers and more pickups and cars as I pulled back onto the highway. After settling down to the speed limit, I started thinking about what David had said in the long telephone conversation we had during his third week in Blue Valley. His manner had been light and happy that week. "Hi, Anne," he had begun, "haven't had time to write this week so I thought I'd call."

It was eleven o'clock on Friday night and I had just come in from a sort of boring date to a dull movie. "I'm so glad you did," I told him. "What's new in the spook department?"

He laughed. "Seems like everybody I talk to up here who'll talk to me at all has a ghost I should meet."

"Well, have you met any?"

He became serious and said, "Not really. I've spent some time looking into a few of the reports about other houses, but none of them seem to be authentic except Goldengrove."

"Your letter last week said that you hoped to go into the house that night," I said. "Did you?"

He seemed to hesitate. "What day did I write that letter? Tuesday?"

"I think so."

"No, I didn't go inside that night. But the next night I prowled around outside the house and finally managed to meet the professor..." He gave a wry laugh. "The *hard* way."

"What do you mean, David?" I asked, disturbed by some odd note in his voice.

"He nearly shot me," he said reluctantly and added hastily, "but I asked for it. I sneaked onto the grounds and he caught me."

"Why did you have to sneak around? Haven't you met this man and talked with him?"

"I've met him now." I could tell he was grinning. "You see, Anne, there have been so many curiosity seekers coming around since his wife died that the professor refuses to see anybody on any matter concerning the house. I couldn't get past his secretary at the university or the maid at his house. I did manage to have a short conversation on the phone with him late one night but he didn't want to cooperate with me."

"That's strange since he was probably once a struggling young Ph.D. candidate himself," I said.

"Exactly my thoughts," he exclaimed. "And I used that approach to try to get through to him."

"With no luck?"

"He softened up enough to tell me that he doesn't live in Goldengrove itself but in the carriage house down the lane a piece. I didn't know at the time that an old relative does live in the big house so I figured I could sort of wander around the place late at night without his knowing I was there."

I was a little surprised, but not much. "But that's trespassing, little brother. Did you see or hear anything?"

"Well, that night," he said, "the first thing I heard was a peacock scream when I stepped on its tail near the back door. So I ran around to the front of the house planning to put my ear to the front door to see if I could hear anything inside. The next thing I heard was a gun being cocked and the professor asking me what I thought I was doing with my ear on his front door."

"What happened then?" I asked.

"Needless to say I hastily assured him that I was only a graduate student, not a burglar. He said he remembered talking with me on the phone. Then he unlocked the front door and led me inside, still with the gun on me, turned on one small lamp and asked to see my identification."

David paused so I insisted that he go on.

"He sort of chuckled and said by damn I was a graduate student."

"I wonder what he expected," I said.

"So do I," David answered. "In fact when I saw him in the light, I almost asked to see his identification."

"Why?"

"Because of what he was wearing." He was quiet a moment. "He had on black slacks, a black sweatshirt with a hood, and black sneakers."

I said, "Humph! That certainly doesn't sound like what the well-dressed professor wears to grade papers."

"Well, not at two o'clock in the morning anyway," David agreed. "But at last I was in Goldengrove."

I was excited for him. "Did you see or hear anything?"

He laughed again. "What I saw was the professor turning out the lamp and what I heard was him saying he hoped some of his graduate students are as persistent as I am. Then he led me to the door."

"Oh, David," I said, "do you mean he didn't let you stay in at all?"

"No," he answered, "but he did leave the front door wide open for a few minutes while we sat on the front steps. He acted as though he was on guard, speaking very softly and stopping occasionally just to listen to the sounds around us. He told me there had been no doubt in his wife's mind that Goldengrove is haunted but that whatever the sounds in the house, he was certain that they are not from malevolent forces."

I sighed. "I'm glad you finally got through to the old fellow, David. Now maybe he will help you."

David laughed again. "I don't know just how much he'll help me, Anne, but he isn't an old fellow. Judging from his looks, I'd guess him to be in his thirties—coal black hair and eyes to match the black outfit, longish hair, in fact. Shorter than I am, but more strongly built."

"He sounds evil-looking to me," I said and shuddered at the thought of David encountering such a man in the dark.

"Oh, come on, sis," he said. "Don't try to make him out a Gothic Romance villain." And he hesitated. "But speaking of romance, the real kind, you should see a fellow I just met today in the library."

"Should I rush right up to little old Blue Valley?" I asked with a laugh.

"Not tonight," he answered. "It's too far, but I did tell him about my good-looking sister in New Orleans. Really, Anne, this fellow might help me. He's a young minister whose church is on ground adjoining Goldengrove. In fact, I understand that his cemetery, which isn't used today, is filled with the original owners of Goldengrove. He's going to help me record names from the headstones."

"How fascinating," I said dryly, "and what's his name?"

"The Reverend Billy Ray Johnson."

"A local boy, I gather."

"How could you tell?"

"By the name. Did you ever know anybody from rural Mississippi who went by just their first name?" I laughed and said, "And I guess he wears a white hat in the drama?"

"But definitely," said David, "over his bright red hair. But if this were a real drama, I guess we'd have to let the two switch roles because Billy Ray has a bad leg and walks with a cane while our black-robed professor walks nimbly around on two good legs."

I remembered that we talked on for a few more minutes about things at home, but I could not remember the mention of any other names in Blue Valley except Miss Allie Collins, the professor's elderly cousin who was living at Goldengrove. David had not gone into any detail at all about what he was doing and certainly said nothing of substance in the other telephone call he had made. But there was a cold prickle down my spine as I tried to think through the situation. I tried to tell myself that everything was all right, but the cold prickle stayed with me nonetheless.

The highway traffic thickened and I realized that Bottom and I were nearing Meridian, Mississippi, which meant we had been on the road nearly four hours and should have three hours to go to reach Blue Valley according to the map I had practically memorized the night before.

I found a service station with a hamburger place next door, and Bottom and I stretched our legs, had a hamburger apiece—with fries—and then after putting up the top of the car, we left the four-lane road we had enjoyed since New Orleans and plunged into the kudzu-covered backroads of north Mississippi. Of course, the roads themselves weren't really covered with kudzu, but everything along the sides of the highway was alive with the ubiquitous vine. A few miles south of Meridian the sky had turned dark and a few miles north a stormy rain started falling on us and kept falling on us all the way to Blue Valley, where there was no kudzu.

Well, we got almost all the way to Blue Valley.

We had just passed a sign informing us that we were five miles from Blue Valley, the *Town with the Past in the Present—Site of Fifty Antebellum Homes*, when I noticed another sign beside a narrow road running off to the right which invited us to visit the *Goldengrove Baptist Church, One Mile Away*.

It was four o'clock. The rain had slowed to a fine drizzle, and the sky had lightened considerably. Curiosity as to just what Goldengrove looked like made me turn around at the next crossroads and go back to the turnoff. I figured it shouldn't take me more than ten minutes to run up the road and look at the house before going on into town. I didn't have a reservation, but I felt I would have no trouble finding a room at the motel where David had been staying.

The road plunged between a row of overlapping, rain-heavy oak trees and down a steep hill over a bridge spanning a small swirling creek. On the other side of the creek, the road was no longer blacktopped, but covered with gravel worn thin in two ruts down the middle. I slowed to a crawl because under the wet gravel the roadbed looked suspiciously like slick red clay. All the turning and changing of speed had disturbed Bottom and he sat up and leaned over to rest his head beside my shoulder. He whined a little.

"Me too, Bottom," I told him. "Maybe we should have waited until tomorrow when we're not so tired to see what Goldengrove looks like."

But since we had come that far, I wanted to press on. Not to mention the fact that there was no place to turn around. And finally we rounded a curve up a hill where the tree tunnel ended and the land was cleared off into neat pasture fields. Ahead up the next hill I could see the little church and beyond it at the top of the rise stood Goldengrove. At that moment the skies suddenly cleared and the sun drifted through the clouds to turn that hill into the prettiest sight I have ever seen: the little white church stood near the road among a few sweetgum trees turned dark orange in this late October and behind it was the small cemetery, a few tall gray-white tombstones within a black iron fence, but beyond that peaceful scene stood a large grove of elm trees turned bright yellow, truly a golden grove from which rose a magnificent white mansion, not of the white columns and wide galleries plantation house type typical of antebellum homes, but reminiscent of some fine French chateau with lacily designed windows behind inset galleries and balconies with its third story a huge hexagonal turret rising majestically above the gabled roof of the second floor.

There was no other traffic on the little road that afternoon so I stopped the car to gaze a moment at the scene before me. It should always be October for Goldengrove, I thought, and pushed back the realization that all the golden leaves would have to fall soon. I was filled with a strange sense of peace at that moment as if all would be well in my world.

Bottom nudged my shoulder with his soft nose

and brought me back to reality and the knot in my stomach came back to remind me I didn't know where David was and that I must push on to be sure of arriving in Blue Valley in time to find a room.

Almost as suddenly as it had appeared, the sun went away and the rain took up where it had left off, only heavier this time. I drove on up the hill, pausing to read the sign in front of the church: *Welcome to Goldengrove Baptist Church, Services on Sunday mornings at eleven and Wednesday evenings at seven, Billy Ray Johnson, Pastor*, and to note the delicate steeple and lovely stained glass windows softly aglow in the stormy haze. There were two cars standing in the churchyard. I eased on by, driving carefully to stay in the well-worn ruts. Some two hundred yards past the church, I came to the cobblestone lane leading up to Goldengrove and could now see the carriage house about halfway between a front gate and the house. The estate was fenced in by a low brick wall broken at this point by the high black iron gate. On the road side of the wall near the gate stood a gnarled old tree whose leaves had already turned dull brown, and whose branches were swaying in the gusty wind that had begun to blow.

I decided to turn around here, figuring there was plenty of room for my little car to swing in and out and we would be on our way to town.

What I didn't count on was that I wasn't accustomed to maneuvering a car through wet gravel and red clay. When I turned, the movement was too sharp and the car spun halfway around and slid to a stop in the mud at the base of that old tree. And judging from the soft crunch I heard, I realized that my front right fender had nudged the tree. I raced the motor and desperately tried to extricate the car from the mud while Bottom softly muttered—with encouragement or from fear, I'm not sure which.

"Well, Bottom," I sighed, "it looks like I'll have to get out and see what I can see." This wouldn't have brought much comment from Bottom if he had been able to talk because he had always hated rain with a passion.

I had a raincoat and umbrella carefully packed in the trunk but nothing except my jacket in the car. I decided I had rather have it wet than to have my new sweater get soaked so I slipped on the jacket and tied a scarf around my head, then opened the door and stepped out into the mud. Luckily I left the car door open behind me; otherwise Bottom couldn't have followed me out after the accident and I might have stayed there in the mud for hours. Just as I reached the front of the car, I heard a loud cracking noise above me and looked up to see what seemed like the whole tree falling on my head. I instinctively threw up my right arm and blacked out as a massive limb crashed down upon me.

I came to—I don't know just how long afterwards—weighted down in the mud and covered by the limb to the sound of Bottom barking, whining, and snarling in turn. Then I heard voices.

One of them said to Bottom, "That's all right, fellow, we see him." And the other voice said, "That dog has the loudest bark I ever heard."

The first voice answered rather rudely, "Thank God for it, I say if you'll pardon my invading your realm."

I tried to move my right arm and the pain was so intense that I passed out again.

When I came to that time, the limb was being dragged off my body and someone was saying, "It's a girl, not a man." And Bottom was trying to push his way in to lick my face, all the while still barking and snarling at the two men.

The other voice said a bit sarcastically I thought, "Are you sure you can manage to lift that side of the branch, Billy Ray?"

"Don't you worry about me, now," answered the other one sweetly. "God helps those who need help. I'll manage." And the oppressive, scratchy mass was off and Bottom was all over me. I was face down and in his enthusiasm the big dog pushed me over onto the hurt arm I was trying to shield and I again blacked out.

"My God, is she dead?" I heard as I came to the next time. "Get that damn dog out of the way so we can see."

The other voice said softly, "Now, Rockford, he's just trying to protect her." And he must have taken a step nearer because Bottom who was crouched over me snarled and snapped at him.

I was cold and wet and my arm hurt. I raised my head and said, "I'm not dead." And to add to the confusion I started weeping. At the sound of my voice, Bottom leaped over to put his head near mine. "It's all right, Bottom," I sobbed.

"Bless her heart," I heard Billy Ray say. Bottom snarled at him again.

The other voice came nearer. "Now cut out that sniffling until we see if you have anything to cry about," it said grumpily. Then, "All right, Bottom, move aside."

And Bottom moved aside and strong arms reached down, turned me over and lifted me up from my left side, luckily since my right arm was crumpled and bleeding.

A hand appeared with a clean white handkerchief and wiped my muddy face and helped me blow my nose, and I looked first into the blackest eyes I had ever seen and then into the bluest. The black eyes were frowning at me and the blue eyes were smiling. Both of the men wore raincoats but water was dripping from their bare heads.

Good old wet Bottom was jumping around doing his best to disengage me from the two men. And I was trying desperately not to throw up. I managed to convince Bottom to calm down and then clenched my teeth to fight the nausea. And to keep them from rattling against each other in my mouth because I couldn't stop shivering.

I noticed through my discomfort that there were two cars parked near mine but on firm roadbed. The professor carrying me toward one of the cars, giving orders as he went: "Get her car keys and purse out of the Fiat and shut the door. Come help me put her into my car."

Billy Ray Johnson limped over to my car and followed the orders without arguing. "Where are you taking her?" he asked as he opened the back door of a black Cadillac.

"Not back there," ordered the professor. "We'll put her in the front and the dog in the back." And he eased me into the car, then took off his raincoat, shook as much of the rain off it as he could, and wrapped it gently around me. He dashed around the car and slid under the wheel while Billy Ray opened the back door for Bottom, who needed no invitation to leap in out of the wet weather.

"I asked you where you're taking her, Rockford," he stated, leaning in over me. I could tell that the two men did not like each other.

"Doc Perkins' office down at the Crossroads."

"Do you want me to come along?" the minister said.

"I can manage," said the other one. "Anyway what are you doing here on Tuesday afternoon? A meeting?"

"Yes," answered the minister. "But I can tell the committee I won't be there and follow you if you want me to."

I realized that I should say something. "Thank you very much for your help, Mr. Johnson, but I don't want you to miss your meeting." I leaned my head against the seat and continued to shiver. "Please, Professor Andrews, take me to the doctor,"

Both men stared at me. I realized then that although we had not introduced ourselves, I had called both of them by name. Perhaps I should have been less open and gone under an assumed name or something, I thought to myself, but I was too much in pain to think deviously.

"I'm Anne Whitehead," I explained, closing my eyes as I talked. "I came up here to look for my brother David, who has mentioned both of you in his calls and letters."

The professor started his car and the minister withdrew his head saying, "I'll call you later, Rockford, to see what the doctor said. I'll find somebody to pull her car out of the mud, too."

I said, "Thanks," and the professor grunted out some sort of reply and we roared off down the road on past Goldengrove.

Bottom shook himself and I winced. "Oh my goodness," I exclaimed weakly, "he'll ruin your car. I am so sorry." And I started crying again. Which embarrassed me because I am not the crying type.

The professor growled at me. I gathered he didn't like tears. "Stop that, I told you. These seats are leather, and we'll be at Doc Perkins' in less than ten minutes."

His tone made me mad. "But I hurt," I said childishly.

"Crying won't help," he retorted. "You'll just upset that dog again. Now hush. What were you doing to get in this fix anyway?"

"Trying to turn around," I answered, sniffing loudly.

He handed me a tissue from the glove compartment. "Blow your nose."

I eased my left hand out from under his raincoat and blew my nose. The movement brought on another wave of nausea so I closed my eyes and concentrated on not being sick the rest of the way.

After a few minutes, I felt the car come to a stop. We were in front of an old-fashioned house which with a small post office, a couple of other houses, and a general store stood at the intersection of the road we were on and a wider blacktopped road.

The rain had slowed to a drizzle and the sky had begun to turn dark for night. "You stay in the car, Bottom," the professor said as he got out. He went around and opened my door. "Do you think you can walk?"

"I think so," I said and I really thought I could, but on standing up, I started blacking out again. When I came to I was once more in the professor's arms inside the doctor's waiting room, and he was explaining to a little pink-cheeked, white-haired gnome of a man what had happened.

"The first thing we have to do is warm her up," said Dr. Perkins, and he called to someone named Maude to bring warm water and towels to the examining room where he had the professor put me on a table. "Now, Collie," he told him, "while Maude and I get her cleaned up, you run over to the store and get Mary Elizabeth to sell you a large soft bathrobe and a big flannel nightgown."

Collie, he called the professor. I concentrated on trying to figure out where that name came from to keep from feeling the pain and cold. But soon, without having asked any questions, the doctor and his nurse Maude had stripped off my ruined pantsuit. The pants were actually in one piece, but

Maude had to cut the jacket off because of the hurt arm, and all of it, even my new white sweater, was muddy and wet. The nurse sponged me off with the warm water and rubbed me gently with soft old towels. She even found a brush and smoothed out my short curls and then wrapped a warm quilt around me to cover my panties and bra which had managed to stay dry.

The doctor came back in with a cup of strong hot tea and helped me drink it. The rest of my time there was sort of a nightmarish blur of the X-ray room and stinging stuff being put on my cuts and scratches and my broken arm being set, but finally the kind doctor and his nurse were through with me and I was in the swaddling clothes the professor had bought from the country store, warm and groggy from a sedative Dr. Perkins had given me. I closed my eyes while they talked.

"Where are you going to take her, Collie?" asked Maude.

"You could take her into town and I'll call the hospital and have her admitted," suggested Dr. Perkins. "I don't want her left alone tonight."

It didn't really matter to me at the moment what they did with me as long as I stayed warm and painless, so I didn't try to join the conversation.

"No," said the professor. "I got the idea that she hasn't been into Blue Valley to check into the motel.

I'll take her back to Goldengrove and let Allie keep her tonight."

"Do you think that's wise with Allie as deaf as she is?" asked the doctor.

"And feeling about you the way she does?" added Maude.

The professor paused. "Just because Allie hates me doesn't mean she is a hard old woman who would turn away a person in the shape this poor little thing is in. And for the last few months someone has been staying in the house, so—"

Maude interrupted, "Do you mean that you managed to talk somebody into staying in that haunted house after dark?" He must have nodded. "Well, I'll declare.'" she exclaimed. "I am really surprised. I just knew that after what happened to Marley you would have more trouble than ever getting help."

Dr. Perkins cleared his throat. "Now, Maude, don't upset Collie talking about his wife."

The professor laughed a bitter laugh—the first laugh, bitter or not, I had heard from him. "Never mind, Doc," he said. "Everybody knows that I hadn't lived in the big house for almost a year before Marley died." Again he paused and then continued as though to himself. "I still can't understand how she turned Allie against me. My own mother's cousin." Then he continued with Maude's answer.

"Oh, Maude, you asked about the woman staying with her. Miss Lucy Green agreed to live in as a sort of companion."

Maude laughed. "That explains it! After teaching fifth grade in Blue Valley for forty years, Miss Lucy couldn't be afraid of anything! She'd spank any ghost that got uppity with her."

"Well," said Dr. Perkins, shifting the conversation, "You'd better get this young lady back to Goldengrove and into bed and see that she gets a light warm supper even if you have to wake her up to make her eat. Tell Allie to keep her in bed tomorrow and I'll try to run up that way to look in on her. It'll also give me an excuse to check on Allie—anybody as much over seventy as she is ought to see the doctor more often than she does."

"All right, Doc," said Collie. "I've already called and told them I'm coming in with her."

I started to sit up to get down off the examining table, but the professor stopped me. "Oh, no you don't!" he said. "I don't want you blacking out on me again."

And he picked me up. I thanked Dr. Perkins and Maude for their wonderful care as they walked out onto the front porch with us.

At the car, we found Bottom calmly lying on the back seat. I commented on that. "Oh, I let him out to run while I was going to the store and then put him back in. He's all right," the professor said, and actually smiled down at me as he backed out to close the door. He returned to the porch to take my bundle of clothes from Maude and put it on the floor of the back seat. "I'11 have them cleaned tomorrow on my way to school and see if somebody at the cleaners can mend your jacket. Maude told me that she was careful to rip down the seam when she cut the sleeve and that somebody could probably fix it for us."

Lightning ripped the black night and thunder roared in the distance as we left the dim lights of the crossroads community and started back through the thick darkness to Goldengrove, this time at a slower pace.

"You should do that more often," I told him.

"Do what?"

"Smile."

"I don't see much to smile about when a kid nearly gets killed by a limb off one of my trees," he complained. "First I almost shoot your brother and then this happens."

"My brother!" I exclaimed groggily. "My brother! I almost forgot him in all this."

"I'm not surprised," he muttered. "But I am surprised your folks would let a kid like you come all the way up here like this."

I yawned, not able to concentrate very well on

what I was saying. "No folks. Just David. And I'll have you know," I yawned again, "that I'm twenty-five years old, two years older'n my brother." I could feel him turn quickly toward me but I was accustomed to people not believing my age. I tried to fight the effects of the sedative. "Have you seen my brother?"

"Not since last week. I thought he must have gone to New Orleans. He was underfoot all the time until this past weekend."

"I think something has happened to him." I turned my head to try to see how he reacted and even in my woozy state could tell that his hands tightened on the steering wheel and that his voice was uneasy when he answered.

"Nonsense," he said in his same old grumpy way.

But somehow the word soothed me and I dropped off to sleep for a few moments. A sharp turn on the road woke me and another thought came to me. "Collie," I said.

"Yes?"

"They called you Collie but Billy Ray Johnson called you Rockford. Why?" I asked, as if it were any of my business.

Again the harsh tone. "My wife called me Rockford because she thought Collie was undignified for a professor." And he leaned forward over the wheel watching the storm-lashed road ahead.

That sedative must have been powerful because having been raised in New Orleans under the threat of hurricanes, I was usually very uneasy in bad weather, but tonight nothing seemed to exist outside that warm car.

"I like Collie," I said foolishly, and saw him glance over at me.

"Go back to sleep," he said gruffly, and I did.

I vaguely remember being lifted from the car and feeling surprised that it wasn't raining on me; there was a sort of carport behind the house at the back door, I learned later. And I distinctly remember the cold shiver that ran through me when a loud voice greeted us at the entrance. "Well, Professor," it said with great scorn, "another one of your women?"

Another voice tried to shush the first one. "Now, Miss Allie, you know I told you he said on the phone that he never saw her before today. She's the sister to that nice young man who's been coming over to talk with us."

"You're sure?" asked the first voice.

"I'm positive," shouted Collie. Then he lowered his voice. "Why didn't you make her put on her hearing aid, Miss Lucy?"

"Who's going to make her do anything?" Miss Lucy stated rather than asked.

"Quit mumbling!" ordered the other one.

I didn't open my eyes and must have dropped off again because the next thing I knew Collie was gently putting me down. I opened my eyes then and managed to focus on the fact that he was laying me on a huge four-poster bed in a golden room. There were soft yellow draperies on the bed, yellow flowers on the wall, and a golden fire in the fireplace. Bottom had followed and was standing beside Collie. I closed my eyes again.

"Please go get the food I asked you to fix," I heard him tell Miss Lucy, whose face I had yet to see and then I heard Collie washing his hands in an adjoining bathroom.

Everything sort of runs together in my mind from then on about that evening. I know that Miss Lucy did come back with a tray of food and that Collie fed me and that they helped me into the bathroom where Miss Lucy stayed with me while I performed the necessary. Then she found a new toothbrush for me to use. They took off the big bathrobe and tucked me in among the yellow sheets and soft blankets. Collie gave me a pill that the doctor had sent. I felt cold again when I realized that he must be about to leave and I grabbed at his hand. "Don't leave me, Collie."

He leaned over and smoothed the hair back from my forehead as if I were a child and said, "I'll be back, Anne. I'll take Bottom out and feed him, and then I'll run over to my place and get some things and be back in no time." He pulled a chair near the bed. "Miss Lucy will sit here with you while I'm gone, won't you, Miss Lucy?"

"Of course I will," she said kindly. "Miss Allie is watching TV downstairs and I can sit here with you, Anne."

"That reminds me," Collie said suddenly. "Anne, you're in a second floor bedroom and the stairs are very steep so don't go wandering about if you wake up later." His voice became stern and abrupt again. "Do you hear me, Anne?" He shook my good shoulder.

"I hear you," I finally answered. "You don't have to shout at me." And then even in my hazy mind I felt ashamed for saying that. "I'm sorry, Collie." I yawned at him and went back to sleep, lulled not only by the medicine but also by the steady beat of the rain on a metal roof somewhere and the soft crackle of the logs burning in the fireplace.

How could this peaceful place be haunted? I thought to myself as I snuggled under the covers. How indeed I was to discover later.

Chapter Two

In my drug-hazy sleep did I dream that there were people talking just outside my door? Dream or fact, the words pierced my conscious mind and stayed with me.

Allie must have put on her hearing aid because the other two were not shouting at her, but neither were they talking in normally quiet tones.

"Are you sure she's all right?" It was Billy Ray Johnson's voice.

Miss Lucy answered. "I'm sure. It's just that Miss Allie thought you should know about it."

"Yes, she was right," he agreed. "I came over as fast as I could."

Miss Allie spoke. "Do you think he saw you?"

"No," he answered, "I didn't drive; I walked over by the back path from the church. Are you sure he won't return for a few minutes?"

"He said he was going to take a shower and eat something, then come back," said Miss Lucy. "He hasn't been gone fifteen minutes yet. I called you the minute he left."

Miss Allie sounded fearful in her next question. "Do you think he did this to that girl?"

Billy Ray was not slow to answer. "No, not at all," he said. "I was there before he arrived at the scene of the accident. There was no way he could have dropped that limb on her."

"Is this one of the women you've seen him with in town, Brother Johnson?" asked Miss Allie, voice trembling with what sounded like anger.

"No, ma'am." Again a quick answer. "I had time to check her wallet for identification before Rockford drove up this afternoon. She really is David Whitehead's sister."

"How did you know she was there in the first place?" asked Miss Lucy.

"That beast of a dog of hers was howling and barking like the end of the world was upon us," he said. "Thank God, or she might have been there for hours. And I could see the car off the road when I looked that way from the door of the church. So I jumped in my car and drove down there to check on things. Rockford must have heard the dog too because, as I told you, he came up from the carriage house right after I arrived on the scene."

"Should we warn her about him since you don't think she is mixed up with him?" asked Miss Allie.

"Not just yet, ladies," he answered. "After all, we must give him the benefit of the doubt as long as we can. We have no proof that he was responsible for Marley's accident and we don't know that he is behind that young man's disappearance. We have to watch and wait and try to find out what he is up to before we make a move."

"Oh, Brother Johnson," said Miss Allie, "you are such a comfort to us. I don't know what we would do without you. But you must put your boots back on and leave before he catches you here." I thought she must be shaking her head. "How could he be so cruel as to tell you never to come in this house again?"

I could imagine him giving her a pastorly pat on the shoulder. "Now, Miss Allie," he said as gently as he could at the volume he had to use, "let's not be unkind. After all, he resented my sweet friendship with Marley. We have enough to worry over about him without adding his hatred of me."

One of them must have opened my door wider and looked in. "Is she still asleep?" asked Miss Lucy.

"Yes," answered Billy Ray Johnson, "but you had best go back in and sit with her. Keep me posted and send for me if I can help. I'll drop by tomorrow to visit her while the professor is at the university."

I don't remember hearing Miss Lucy come back into my room.

I do remember waking up later. How much later I couldn't tell, but I knew it had to be past midnight because the fire had died out completely and the house was still. Strangely enough, I did not feel disoriented. I knew where I was in spite of the sedative and also I felt wide awake at once. It was almost as if someone had called my name.

I moved about a bit in the bed to check my aches and pains and heard Bottom yawn. Collie had let him bed down on the pale gold carpet near my bed. I let my good left arm fall down over the edge of the bed to scratch his head, but realized that the four-poster was too high up in the air for me to reach him lying down so I patted the cover and he at once stood up on his hind legs and laid his head on my stomach. I lay there a few minutes scratching his ears and listening to the distant thunder while intermittent flashes of lightning broke through the draperies at the one big window in the room near the head of my bed. As the window would glow, the room would come to life with shadows, and I tried to pick out what each one was—the rocking chair where Miss Lucy had sat, the marble-topped washstand complete with brightly flowered pitcher and bowl, the huge armoire, the fireplace and the big blue wing chairs on each side of it, the open door to the bathroom and the closed door to the hall.

The storm was gathering momentum again and at first I thought the noise was a part of it. So sure was I that the wind was singing in the elm grove that I decided to go to the window and watch the big golden trees swaying in the wind when the lightning flashed.

Aside from the twinges in my arm and the dull ache in my head, I felt surprisingly good as I swung my feet over the side of the bed and groped for the bedstep. Bottom shook himself with a soft rattle of his collar tags and followed me to the window, which I found to be actually French doors that opened onto a small balcony where the rain was making soft plops in the puddles of water collected out there.

In spite of my flannel nightie, I found myself a bit chilly so I stepped behind the heavy curtains and let them fall about my shoulders as I waited for lightning flashes.

Bottom nudged his way into the curtains and leaned against me. The singing grew louder and a series of long jagged streaks in the sky lighted the golden grove. The whining notes rose and fell in my ears, but not a leaf was moving in the elm trees. The wind had stopped blowing.

I knelt beside Bottom and put my good arm around him. I peered out the panes of glass through the lacy ironwork of the balcony railing trying to focus on just one tree to be sure my eyes were not playing tricks on me. In the next flash I again saw that not a branch stirred in that tree except where the raindrops were trickling down.

The singing became almost a definite tune and crescendoed to the point that we were surrounded by it. I had the feeling there was movement of some kind in the room behind us. I tightened my grip on Bottom and he licked my hand, seemingly undisturbed by what was going on.

The ghosts. I had somehow forgotten the ghosts. Were they looking for me?

Suddenly the sound became softer, almost a whisper but with a definite shape of words now. I strained to understand and thought I heard my name. Over and over the voices seemed to be saying the same thing:

"Anne, go home." "Anne, go home." "Anne, go home."

The words, or at least what I thought were words, beat against my ears over and over until I could stand it no longer. A thunder bolt crashed nearby, Bottom whined, and I screamed.

The singing stopped.

In the hush that followed, footsteps clattered

along the uncarpeted hallway and someone rushed into my room and turned on the overhead light.

It was Collie. "Anne, what's—" he began and stopped short. All of my strength was exhausted. I couldn't make myself rise and come from behind the curtains.

I heard him fling open the bathroom door and rush through to Miss Lucy's room, which opened off the other side of the bathroom. I heard him say sternly, "I thought I told you to leave those two doors open. Anne's not in her bed."

As he came back, Bottom thumped his tail. Collie whispered, "My God, the balcony," and flung the curtains open.

"I'm right here, Collie," I managed to say and started trying to stand up, a feat in itself difficult in my voluminous nightgown.

He reached down and lifted me roughly to my feet.

"What are you doing down there?" he shouted angrily. But when I raised my eyes and looked into his, I saw a mixture of terror and concern that did not match the tone of his voice.

I raised my free hand and laid it against his cheek, then said softly, "I'm all right, Collie. Bottom and I were just watching the storm."

Behind him, Miss Lucy bustled into the room pulling a flowered wrapper around her tall, gaunt figure. "What in the world is going on?" she demanded.

I explained to her and she made some sort of remark to the effect that that had been a dumb thing to do, and then she said indignantly to Collie, "And I did leave those two doors open, Professor. The draft must have closed them."

What draft, I wondered, beginning to shiver.

"I'm sorry, Miss Lucy," Collie told her. "I didn't mean to shout at you."

"Humph!" she snorted. "You haven't changed much since the fifth grade." But she said it almost affectionately. It made me wonder whose side she was on.

She tucked me back under the covers, and Collie told her to go back to bed. "I'll light the fire and sit here and read until Anne goes back to sleep."

"Well, I don't know…" She hesitated.

"Oh, come on, Miss Lucy," he laughed. "We'll leave the doors open, and if I attack her, she'll scream for you."

She gave a little half-smile but propped the door open with a book as she went back to her room.

Silently I watched Collie add some logs to the andirons and start up the fire. The storm had finally roared on over us, and the rain was now steady and calm.

Collie turned on a reading lamp beside one of

the wing chairs and stretched his bare feet toward the fire as he sat down to read a book that was in the pocket of his robe. My last thought before falling asleep was that surely a man who wears a white bathrobe with a book in its pocket and goes barefoot couldn't be all bad.

Suddenly the ghost voices were around me again, and I was weeping from terror partly, but mostly from frustration at not knowing where to find David or how to go about saving him from this unnamed danger that the voices were suggesting.

And then Collie was sitting on my bed cradling me in his arms.

"You were having a nightmare," he said against my hair. "It's all right now."

"It was the ghosts singing again," I shuddered.

"Again?"

"Yes, that's why I screamed earlier. The room was filled with singing while I was behind the curtains."

"Tell me about it," he said softly.

I was torn between the fear that somehow he was responsible for David's disappearance and the feeling he was my only hope of finding my brother. So I didn't tell him about the conversation I had heard earlier but I did tell him why I was behind the curtains and what the voices seemed to say in their song.

"Are you sure you didn't hear them?" I asked, pulling away from him to look into his face.

He shook his head. "I only heard you scream." He put a hand on each of my shoulders and spoke firmly: "The so-called ghost voices are only the sounds of wind caught in an old ventilating system. The words were your own psychological interpretation of those sounds."

I wanted to believe him, especially since my shoulders burned under his hands and my eyes read concern, not malice, in his gaze.

He stood up and gently tucked me in again, never taking his eyes from mine. Then he leaned over and kissed me and I knew that whatever he was, I was very attracted to Professor Rockford Collins Andrews.

"Now go to sleep," he said gruffly and went back to his chair. Bottom stretched out at his feet, and I had no more nightmares that night.

Somewhere a clock was striking nine o'clock when I woke up the next morning. Also, I could hear the comfortable sounds of a carpet sweeper's hum and a radio broadcaster's voice assuring the Blue Valley area that the rains were over and done with and the sun was here to stay for a few days. The volume lowered as he announced that the Morning Musical Medleys would now resume.

I sat up—achey in head, shoulders and arm, but otherwise in one piece—swung my legs off the bed, and climbed down. On a bench at the foot of the bed stood my suitcase and in the bathroom I found my makeup kit. After doing as much of my daily morning bathroom routine as I could with one hand, I went to the French doors and pulled open the curtains.

I could hardly believe the beauty of the elm grove. The wind and rain had laid a carpet of golden leaves over the ground under the trees but had not by far stripped the elegant elms of their fall dress. The morning sun softly lighted the world outside and sparkled on the steeple of the little church next door and on the brilliantly colored trees around it. As if cued to enter at that moment, a peahen strolled into view out front followed by a peacock in full-feather strut.

"I can't believe it!" I exclaimed aloud.

"Can't believe what?" asked Miss Lucy coming in followed by Bottom who rushed over to nuzzle my good hand. She was carrying a tray of food.

"This scene," I said. "I've never seen anything so beautiful."

She came over and joined me at the window.

"It is lovely," she agreed. "But get back in bed and eat your breakfast before it gets cold."

"I hate to put you to all this trouble—" I began, but she shushed me, so I crawled back into the big old bed and let her set the tray on my lap.

In spite of having only one hand at my disposal, I had no trouble getting rid of the delicious food: hot biscuits already buttered, blueberry preserves, sausage, scrambled eggs, and a little silver pot of *café au lait*. Miss Lucy sat in the rocker and chatted while I ate. She told me that Brother Johnson had pulled my car out of the mud the day before and left it at the professor's carriage house, and this morning he (the professor) had brought it up to the garage and had sprayed it with a waterhose to check the damage—which was slight—and then he had brought in my bags. He had also taken the dog out for a run and fed him before leaving for the university. He sent word that his last class would be over at one and that he would come directly home after that. I was not to worry about anything at all but was to lie still and rest all day as Doc Perkins had directed. Miss Lucy talked on and on in what was supposed to be a cheerful manner, but somehow the cheerfulness was forced and when I glanced up from my concentrated efforts to eat, I saw that her eyes were worried and her manner tense. She was gripping the arms of the rocking chair as she rocked and her rocking was erratic and jerky. When she saw that I had almost finished, she stood up to take the tray.

"Miss Allie and Brother Johnson would like to come up to visit with you," she said. "He dropped by to check on you."

"How nice of him," I said lightly, somehow not wanting any of them to know I had heard their conversation last night. "But give me time to brush my teeth and put on my bathrobe. I couldn't entertain the preacher in my nightgown."

She smiled and carried the tray of empty dishes out. I found that the sleeves of my new bathrobe were large enough for my cast to slip through and while not at all glamorous looking, the robe did cover me modestly and its soft red color made me look more lively than I felt because the more Miss Lucy had talked, the more my spirits had drooped until by now I was dreading what I feared the three of them planned to say about Collie. Bottom sensed my unease and came to stand near me.

The dog stiffened and muttered in his throat as we heard footsteps outside the door. I called "Come in" to the gentle tapping on the door.

Billy Ray Johnson entered alone but left the door open behind him. Bottom growled as the preacher limped toward the bed where I was sitting.

"Good morning, Miss Whitehead," said the

handsome young man.

"Good morning, Mr. Johnson," I replied, smiling at him while hanging onto Bottom.

"You have a good chaperone there, Anne," he laughed. Then he addressed Bottom as he stopped near the foot of the bed. "Don't worry, pup. Miss Allie and Miss Lucy will be up in just a minute."

"I can't imagine why he's acting like this," I apologized, but suddenly I did know: I remembered that this man had gone through my purse which was lying on the front seat of my car. Had he hit Bottom in the process? For surely Bottom would object to a stranger messing around with my things especially when he was upset over my being under that limb.

I decided I'd best change the subject. "Your church looks lovely with the fall leaves around it," I said.

"Yes, it does," he agreed. "I guess you're not used to seeing the fall colors in New Orleans."

"Not much. Most of our trees stay green all year," I said and was glad to hear the two ladies coming along the hallway.

"Good morning, young lady," said Miss Allie kindly as she bustled into the room, a short soft woman wearing a blue dress that complemented her fair skin and snowy hair. I was relieved to see that she was wearing her hearing aid. Miss Lucy followed close behind her and they too came to stand near my bed.

"You are very kind to take me in like this, Miss Allie," I said sincerely. "I do appreciate."

"We are glad to have you, child," she said, "glad to have you."

"Won't you all sit down?" I suggested, feeling rather like something on display as the three of them stood there looking down at me, obviously not sure how to begin telling me what I knew they felt their duty to say.

"No, we'll stand," said Miss Allie. "It's almost ten o'clock."

"Yes," said Miss Lucy, "but it's Wednesday, Allie, remember?"

"Oh, Wednesday," Miss Allie repeated, obviously relieved. "Then he has a twelve o'clock class."

"Yes," said Billy Ray, "but even so we must be careful. He could dismiss that class today."

They drew nearer the bed and I lay back on the pillows, looking from one to the other of them, afraid for them to begin talking. Afraid of what they might convince me when they did.

"We must ask you some questions and tell you some things," said Miss Allie.

"All right," I answered.

Billy Ray Johnson took over. "Anne, had you ever seen Rockford Andrews before yesterday?"

"Never," I replied and added, "nor had I seen any of you before either. Why?"

He ignored my question. "Did your brother write you or communicate with you in any way about any irregularities he might have stumbled on around here?"

"No," I said after pausing a moment to think. "Why?"

Again no answer to my question. Instead, he leaned nearer me and gazed deeply into my eyes. "When did you last hear from him?"

"He called me Saturday night," I said, feeling all at once as if I didn't really want to discuss my brother with these people.

"Did he mention the professor?" asked Miss Lucy.

"No," I said, looking into her worried eyes.

"You see, Allie," she said, "we can't blame Collie when we have no proof."

The preacher gestured impatiently and resumed. "What did he say that made you come up here to look for him"

"Nothing, really," I said, reluctant for some reason to tell him what David had said. "He just sounded strange and when I tried to call him back on Sunday, the motel manager said he had checked out."

No one spoke.

"Oh," I added, "the motel manager said David had told her he would be staying with a friend so I was hoping he was at your house, Billy Ray."

"Why?" he asked.

"Because he spoke of you earlier saying he thought you could help him."

"Well," sighed the preacher, "I wish I could help, but I'm afraid we have to tell you that your brother has disappeared."

I must have turned pale.

Miss Allie said, "Are you sure she is strong enough today to hear all this?"

I shook my head. "I was afraid of something like that, but I hated to admit it." I looked around at their concerned faces. "Where could he be?" I whispered.

"We don't know, my dear," answered Miss Lucy, "but we do want to help you find him."

"Anne," said Billy Ray, "can you tell us what David was looking for?"

I looked at him blankly. "Ghosts," I finally said.

"I mean besides ghosts."

"Nothing but ghosts," I insisted, "He's doing research for his doctoral dissertation. He heard Goldengrove is haunted and came to check it out."

Billy Ray straightened up and the three of them looked at one another.

Then I asked him a question of my own. "Why do you and Collie Andrews hate each other?"

His answer was quick. "I don't hate him, but he does hate me." He lowered his eyes, looking embarrassed. "Somehow he got the notion I was having an affair with his wife."

"Were you?" I asked innocently.

Miss Allie was shocked. "Miss Whitehead," said she indignantly, "Brother Johnson is a Baptist minister."

Miss Lucy said nothing.

The minister bowed his head and folded both hands over the head of his cane. "I was falsely accused, my dear," he said and raised wounded eyes to meet mine. I couldn't help feeling there was also a wicked twinkle in those blue eyes, but I smiled sweetly and told him that I was indeed sorry. Which didn't help matters much, because I could tell he was wondering just what I was sorry about: that he had been falsely accused or that he had not had an affair with the professor's wife.

"Well," said Miss Lucy firmly, her crisp tone breaking the tableau, "best we get on with our purpose."

Billy Ray glanced in her direction and cleared his throat. "Yes," he agreed.

"Miss Whitehead," said Miss Allie, "we feel it our duty to tell you that things are not always as they seem with my cousin."

"Oh?" I asked raising my eyebrows, defensive for Collie, but still curious.

Billy Ray spoke next. "You must be extremely cautious in dealing with Professor Andrews."

"But why?" I insisted. "I keep asking 'Why?' to your odd statements and you keep ignoring me, Billy Ray. Will you please tell me why I should be cautious in dealing with a man who has been nothing but kind to me?"

During this speech I sat up in bed and extended my hand toward him in a gesture of appeal. He came closer, leaned his cane against the bed and took my hand in both of his. Bottom remained on guard but did not object. The man's hands were warm and strong and his grip firm. In my confusion I clung to them. "Please help me," I begged.

"We'll all help you, Anne," he assured me. "But you must be careful."

"My brother. Do you know anything about what has happened to him?" I asked.

"Nothing," he stated flatly and shook his head. "I had invited David to move into my spare room at the parsonage across the road from the church since he was eager to be out here nearer Goldengrove."

"Did he move in?" I asked.

"No," put in Miss Allie loudly, "before he could move in he just disappeared."

Miss Lucy added, "He was out here working until early Saturday morning and as he left, he told us he planned to move into Brother Johnson's house Saturday afternoon and wanted permission to roam around the grounds at night. He went out the back door and over the back path toward the church where he said his car was parked—"

"Yes, he came by to assure me he would move in that afternoon," said Billy Ray.

"And we haven't seen him since," finished Miss Allie.

"Has he phoned either place?" I asked.

"No," said Miss Allie and the other two shook their heads.

"Has Collie heard from him?"

They looked at one another. "He says he hasn't," said Miss Allie, "but we aren't sure."

"Why?" I asked.

"Well," she hesitated, then rushed on, "Brother Johnson thinks he saw David and Collie talking together Saturday afternoon."

"Where?" I asked, withdrawing my hand from Billy Ray's so he wouldn't feel my palm perspiring.

He picked up his cane and moved back a bit. "In front of the post office downtown in Blue Valley. I was driving past and it looked like they were quarreling about something. Rockford was holding one of David's arms while he was trying to pull away."

"And—" I urged.

"That's all," he said. "By the time I found a parking place and walked back to the post office, they had both gone. I was expecting David to move in by five and when he hadn't shown up at six, I called the motel." He paused.

"Go on," I said.

"I was told he had checked out about eleven o'clock that morning."

"But what makes you think Collie is involved?" I asked. "Maybe they had just met by accident."

Again the exchange of glances. Then Miss Lucy spoke. "Collie has been acting strangely for several weeks, Anne. We hate to tell you and we hate to believe bad of him, but we feel we must warn you to be careful."

Miss Allie snorted. "Lucy is being too nice. We have reason to think Collie Andrews is mixed up in something evil."

"Why, Miss Allie," I said, shocked, "he is your own cousin."

She stood up taller. "I can't help it if he is my own flesh and blood, something is wrong." She leaned over and lowered her voice. "We don't have any proof yet, but we fear he had something to do with his wife's death."

"Not all of us," interjected Miss Lucy firmly. "I feel sure there is an explanation for his actions."

Miss Allie turned on her. "An explanation for those foreign-looking women Brother Johnson has seen him with in town? For all that running around at night in those black clothes? For all that ghost singing talk—"

"Now, Miss Allie," the minister said, "you know that people have believed forever that Goldengrove is haunted. He certainly didn't start that."

"Yes, but Marley said the sounds had changed," she insisted, "and I think that he had something to do with whatever was going on."

"Did David hear the ghosts before he disappeared?" I asked, suddenly feeling weak and frightened.

"Yes," Miss Lucy said. "I told you he was out here until about one o'clock. He was up on the third floor and he came down terribly excited saying he had heard something."

"We were watching a movie on TV," added Miss Allie, "so I didn't pay too much attention to the young man, but I do remember he was very elated as he left."

"What night was that?" I asked.

"Let's see.'" She thought a bit. "It started on Friday night."

"Yes," said Miss Lucy. "It was Friday night turned into early Saturday morning because as I let him out the back door, he said something about having to wait till Monday to do something because the next day—well, it was already the next day then— was Saturday. We had thought he wanted to spend the whole night in the trunk room that night but it turned out he didn't."

I leaned my head back against the headboard and closed my eyes. My mind was whirling. Could Collie be involved in something that had brought danger to my brother? Miss Allie was talking but I tuned in in the middle of a sentence.

"—and at church Sunday Brother Johnson asked us if we had seen or heard from the young man so we started comparing notes. Brother Johnson was such a comfort to me when Marley died—and to Marley during her last unhappy year."

I opened my eyes and saw her beaming at him.

"Not as much as I'd have liked," he murmured. "If it hadn't been for Rockford's insane accusations I could have helped Marley—and you—so much more." He bowed his head a moment then sighed and looked at me. "Anyway," he continued briskly, "as you can see, Anne, we are concerned about this man's actions and beg you to be careful. As long as your brother didn't tell you anything incriminating about him—" It was a question.

I shook my head weakly in reply.

"—then you should be safe," he went on. "But

if anything strange happens, come to me at once and let me help you."

"If I don't find David tomorrow, I'll have to go to the police," I said. "I'm hoping he just went to investigate another house somewhere."

"Oh, I should have told you," said Billy Ray. "I went to the sheriff on Monday and asked him to be on the lookout for him and I also checked the hospital."

"Why didn't you call me?" I asked.

"He hadn't mentioned you to me," he answered simply. "But now I must run. I've stayed too long already."

"Thank you, Billy Ray," I said and closed my eyes again.

The three of them left Bottom and me alone and I was lying there willing my brain to sort out what I had heard when suddenly a thought brought me upright in the bed.

Billy Ray Johnson had lied to me. I vividly remembered David's telling me he had told the minister about his good-looking sister in New Orleans.

"Oh, well," I decided, "he just forgot about it. Anyway, ministers aren't supposed to lie."

And I dismissed everything from my mind, propped my broken arm on a pillow and went to sleep, suddenly worn out.

Chapter Three

My nap was deep and dreamless and I woke up at
one-thirty to another procession entering my room.
This time Doc Perkins replaced Billy Ray Johnson
in the trio and Miss Lucy was bearing my lunch: a
big bowl of thick steaming soup, a pot of tea, and an
apple turnover.

"Hello, Miss Annie," said the doctor, his pink
face smiling, "I see they're doing right by you."

"They really are," I agreed sincerely.

He looked at the tray. "Just set that down on the
table, Miss Lucy, while I check Annie over. It won't
get cold." He sniffed the soup, "And while I do
this, you and Miss Allie go downstairs and fix me a
bowl of that soup and one of those do-dads there,
but I'll have milk with mine, and I'll be right down
to eat it."

The two old ladies smiled at me and left the

room to follow the doctor's orders.

"Now, young lady," he said, putting his bag beside me, crawling up on the bedstep, and turning around to sit on the bed, "how do you feel?"

"Bruised and confused," I said seriously.

Suddenly we heard a whistling sound from downstairs and Collie calling Bottom. The dog bounded from the room.

"Bruised I can understand," said Doc Perkins, watching Bottom exit. He turned back to look closely at me. "But what is this 'confused' business?"

I twisted the belt to my bathrobe and fought back the tears that were choking me. "It's my brother," I said. "I don't know where he is and I must find him."

"I know," he said, his voice kind. "But for now, look out the window."

I looked out and saw Bottom racing around in the carpet of golden leaves, chasing sticks Collie was throwing for him. I looked back at the doctor.

"Collie told me about your brother and he also told me that he is doing all he can to help you." He patted my hand. "We'll all help you."

I looked away and two big tears slid down my cheeks. "I just don't know which way to turn or who I can trust."

"Trust everybody a little bit and nobody a lot until you are sure of your ground," he said solemnly.

I laughed at his serious expression which did not match the rosy face. "Doc Perkins the philosopher?"

"Something like that," he said without a smile on his face and opened his bag.

I lay still while he checked me over. When he had finished, I asked when I could get up and out.

"You can get up for a while later today but wait until tomorrow morning to do anything strenuous and try to take a nap tomorrow," he said, getting off the bed. He put my lunch tray on my lap and picked up his bag. "I have calls to make all around the area and I'll ask about your brother. Maybe someone has seen him."

"Thank you," I said simply.

"And let me look at your bruises on Friday." He smiled at me and I felt I could trust him more than a little bit. As he was leaving the room, he almost collided with the professor and Bottom.

"Is she all right, Doc?" asked Collie, letting him pass by.

"She'll do, boy," he said. "She'll do." He disappeared around the hallway.

The professor brought in a whiff of the cool autumn air with him and looked boyish with his hair rumpled and his tie loosened under a dark tweed jacket. He came to stand beside me and looked into my face.

His black eyes grew solemn. "You've been crying," he said with a frown.

"Just a little," I admitted. "I can't help being worried about David and frustrated about not being able to look for him."

He softened. "I'm sorry, Anne," he said. "It's just that I hate tears."

"Why?" I asked.

"Because I don't trust them. I've seen too many lies covered by tears." His mouth tightened and he reached down to scratch Bottom's head. "But here," he said suddenly, "you must be starving." He rushed into the bathroom and washed his hands, then came back to watch me eat my lunch, insisting on cutting the turnover and cheering me on in my efforts to use my left hand to feed myself. When Bottom realized that there would be no tidbits for him, he went over in front of the French door and stretched out in the little bit of sunshine drifting in.

"Thank you for taking care of him," I told Collie.

He smiled and looked fondly at the big black and white animal on his golden carpet. "Well, if it hadn't been for Bottom, you might still be lying under that limb off my tree," he said, "so I guess we both owe him something."

He reached over to pick up my tray of empty

dishes and our eyes met and held for a long moment. During that time, my mind kept repeating Dr. Perkins' advice to trust nobody a lot, but my heart was telling me that anybody as nice to me and to Bottom as Collie could not be the villain of the tales I was being told in this house. I fear that my heart was showing in my eyes because he was leaning over the tray to kiss me when Miss Lucy bustled in and broke up the scene.

"Here, I'll take that tray," she said. "I declare, that Doc Perkins beats all: I thought he was going to sit there and eat all afternoon."

"He likes your soup, Miss L," said Collie, handing her the tray and giving a little shrug at me.

"So did I," I said. "Do you do the cooking, Miss Lucy?"

She looked pleased. "Allie and I share the cooking chores and there is a cleaning woman who comes in three days a week to do everything else."

"You've probably heard her clattering around today," Collie said. "She's here on Monday, Wednesday, and Friday and at my place Tuesday and Thursday. She works fast in the house because she is afraid of the ghosts, so if you see a streak flash by, it's she doing her work."

I laughed, the terror of the night before far away. "But I thought the ghosts only sang at night."

"So they do," nodded Miss Lucy, "but we can't

convince Caroline of that."

"If she's afraid, why does she work here?" I asked.

"She has worked here since she was a child and her husband is in charge of the grounds," answered Collie. "I don't think she is really all that afraid. It's sort of a game with her now."

"Or it was," said Miss Lucy pointedly.

I looked at Collie and he lowered his eyes. "My wife mentioned the ghosts just before she died. Caroline and Marley's cook heard her. The cook quit immediately but Caroline was more sensible."

I changed the subject. "Doc Perkins said I can get up later this afternoon."

"Fine," Collie said, and Miss Lucy gave a little smile.

"Come away now, young man," she said to him, "and let Anne rest for a while so she'll feel like getting up later."

"All right," he said. "I'll go change clothes and come back to see you don't overdo."

Bottom stood up a moment not sure whether to go or stay then decided not to leave me. He yawned and stretched then lay back down and closed his eyes. I wiggled lower into the bed and closed mine, too, and set off a series of figures marching through my mind in a confused jumble. Surely there was some sense to all I had seen and heard from David and from all these people who had crowded into my life, but at the moment I could make nothing match anything else. I knew I had to go to Blue Valley as soon as possible to try to find every trace of my brother. I felt that once I had been able to see where he had been, I would be able to project where he might have gone from there. I guess it gave me comfort to think perhaps he had left a trail of pebbles or cookie crumbs or something for me to follow.

There was a gentle knock at my door, and as I called an invitation to enter, a small black middle-aged woman came in with a carpet sweeper in one hand and a feather duster in the other.

"I'm Caroline," she said giving me a shy smile.

"I'm Anne," I answered, smiling back.

"I'll just dust up the room a little if it won't bother you," she said and closed the door.

"I don't mind," I assured her, and she leaned the sweeper against a chair and began wielding the duster with great haste. "You don't have to rush so, Caroline," I said. "Really, you won't bother me at all."

She looked at me quickly and then glanced around the lovely room. "I don't stay in these upstairs rooms any more than I have to," she stated.

"Why?" I asked and saw her eyes dart to the corners of the room again. "Because of the ghosts?"

Her eyes came back slowly to meet mine, and she moved closer to the bed. She was looking at me as if she weren't sure whether or not she wanted to talk with me, and I was impressed with the intelligence in her expression. I knew at once that she was neither ignorant nor uninformed. Finally she spoke. "Yes, because of the ghosts." She had decided not to trust me with whatever she had to say, and I suddenly felt that I had to win her confidence.

"Did my brother David talk to you?" I asked, sitting up.

"About what?" she countered coming over to dust the nightstand.

"About ghosts," I answered, "or about anything. You see, I don't know where he is. He seems to have disappeared." My eyes filled and I had to stop talking. I reached for a tissue from the box on the nightstand. "I'm sorry. I guess having David lost and then being hurt myself is getting to me."

"I understand," she said and stood looking at me for a moment. "He did ask me some questions about the ghosts and I saw him around here several times."

"When did you see him last?"

"Last Friday when I was working, he was here talking with Miss Allie. In fact, I saw him in this very room. I walked by going in to clean up Miss Lucy's room and heard them in here and glanced in the door. He was standing over by the fireplace saying something about wishing he could spend the night in the house."

"You didn't talk to him that day yourself?" I asked, holding the elbow of my broken arm with my left hand. The cast was beginning to feel heavy.

"No, not that day," she answered and changed the subject. "Do you have a sling for that arm?"

I told her that I thought the doctor had sent one home with me (home?), so she looked in the armoire drawers and found the canvas sling which she brought over and helped me put on, adjusting it and fastening it securely around my neck. Then she plumped my pillows and stacked them behind me so that I could lean back comfortably.

"Did you ever hear the ghosts sing, Caroline?" I asked as she started pushing the sweeper across the carpet.

"Just once when I was a child," she answered.

"Do you think there are really such things as ghosts?"

She stopped pushing the sweeper and leaned on the handle. "I think there are really such things as the noises you hear in this house," she said, "but they don't scare me like some of the things I hear from the living."

The tone of her voice sent shivers up my spine, but at that moment we heard someone coming along the passageway and Caroline shook her head as if warning me not to say anything else and went on with her cleaning. She pushed the sweeper over toward the door and opened it in answer to a soft knock. Miss Lucy marched in, her thin back straight, with a glass of iced tea and some teacakes for me.

I couldn't remember seeing teacakes since I was a child. David and I would go every summer to spend two weeks with Mama's Great Aunt Ellen on her farm in south Mississippi, and she always made great batches of the big biscuity teacakes for us to eat with our milk. I bit into one of the tender lemony treats and sighed. "Miss Lucy, you take me back to my childhood with these teacakes."

She was pleased. "That's just exactly what your brother said," she exclaimed. She smoothed the skirt of her dress underneath as she sat down in the rocker and with feet close together gently rocked, watching me eat.

Caroline gathered up her duster and sweeper and eased out of the room, giving me a solemn little smile as she left. Bottom pulled his furry body up and followed her out. What had she been trying to tell me or who was she warning me about? And why did she not want to talk in front of Miss Lucy? My mind kept trying to sort out what was going on and something kept nagging, a feeling that something important had been said or that hadn't yet registered, something that could help me find David.

Was I reading ridiculous hidden meanings into simple things that never harbored hidden meanings? Why was the Reverend Billy Ray Johnson so involved in the goings-on at Goldengrove? Why did Miss Allie distrust her own cousin? Had someone misled her into thinking him bad? If so, who? Had she turned to Billy Ray in desperation or was he only showing neighborly concern for the two old ladies? Why did he and Collie hate each other so obviously? If his wife had believed that the ghosts were really there and that they had something to do with her death, why was Collie so convinced that there was nothing evil about them? What would have happened to me if I had not been out of my bed when the ghosts were in my room the night before? Was I beginning to believe in ghosts myself? I who had argued with David for years that there was no such thing? And behind everything, where was David? And how would I ever find him with my arm broken and my body aching?

I realized that Miss Lucy had been making small talk. "I'm sorry, Miss Lucy," I said when it seemed that she had said something that required an answer. "I didn't hear you."

She stopped rocking and leaned toward me, lowering her voice. "I said that Billy Ray Johnson called earlier and said that when you feel like getting out to let him know if you need him to drive you into Blue Valley." She glanced toward the door. "But don't tell Collie—I think I hear him coming up the stairs."

"Miss Lucy," I said wearily, "I just don't understand all this 'Don't tell Collie' business. How could that man be as bad as you people hint?"

She lowered her voice still more until it became a whisper. "He has a vicious temper at times," and then added mysteriously, "but I believe that at those times he is usually justified. But don't tell Allie I said that."

And now another "Don't tell somebody."

Caroline had left the door open so the professor did not have to knock. He had changed into faded jeans and a white sweatshirt and when he come over close to the bed to greet me, I again smelled the freshness of the outdoors. He ignored Miss Lucy. "I've been running with Bottom," he said. "Do you feel better?"

"I feel tired of this bed," I answered, suddenly thinking I absolutely had to be up and about. I set my tea glass on the nightstand and reached for my bathrobe on the foot of the bed. Miss Lucy helped me put my good arm into one sleeve and drape the other side over the broken arm, cast, sling and all. Then she tied the belt for me. I slipped my feet into the slippers someone had found in my suitcase. Collie came around and gently led me over to one of the wing chairs.

"Where is Bottom now?" I asked, wondering why he hadn't followed Collie up. "I'd be afraid for a city dog like him to be out in the woods alone."

He laughed. "Don't you worry about Bottom. He can take care of himself. But I left him in the kitchen with Caroline. I think he was trying to con her out of something to eat."

"There's some dog food in my car."

"I found it," he assured me. He sat down in the other wing chair.

In the distance we heard Miss Allie calling Miss Lucy. She hesitated, a disgusted expression on her face. "Now how does she expect me to be in two places at once?" she muttered. "She told me to stay with Anne until time to put supper on the table and now she's yelling for me to come back downstairs."

"I'll be all right, Miss Lucy," I told her. "And I'd like to go downstairs for supper if you don't mind."

She looked relieved. "That will be fine," she said. "Supper will be ready at six o'clock." She carefully propped the hall door open with a book and left the room, taking my tea tray with her.

I laughed. "She doesn't trust you, Professor Andrews. Or maybe she doesn't trust me."

He didn't laugh. Instead he leaned over and put his face into both hands, rubbed his eyes and sighed heavily. Then he put one hand on each knee and straightened up to look at me. "It's not you, Anne," he said seriously. "But tell me, do you trust me?"

I was shaken by the intensity of his voice and tried to lighten the mood. "Any friend of Bottom's is a friend of mine," I assured him.

He stood and taking me by the elbows pulled me to my feet so that we were standing close together. He held my face gently in both his hands and looked at me. "Please believe me, Anne," he whispered hoarsely. "No matter what you hear or what happens, I am your friend and I'm trying to help you."

I could not tear my gaze from those black eyes under heavy brows knitted together now into almost a scowl. I lifted my left hand and smoothed the wrinkles out of his forehead and pushed back the lock of softly waving black hair that had fallen onto his face. "I believe you, Collie," I whispered back to him. I meant what I said.

And when he kissed me I felt that truly I had come home to Goldengrove.

I had supper in the kitchen with my two hostesses

and then stayed downstairs for a while watching television with them in the little room off the kitchen they called the sunroom. But when a local country music show started, I excused myself and went back upstairs.

Collie had left just before the meal saying he would eat a sandwich later but that he had some work to do until around nine. Bottom raced up the stairs ahead of me and was waiting at the door of my room. I had found on leaving the room, as I had been told, that the passageway outside was not an ordinary hall but a balcony looking down on the marbled entryway and up to the third floor balcony and the skylight beyond that.

There were four doors opening onto the second floor balcony and a wide hallway centering a wing toward the back of the house. The whole house was blazing with lights so I walked on past my door and Miss Lucy's and turned down the hallway. There were three rooms besides Miss Lucy's off this passageway and at the end a narrow stairway leading downstairs. I could hear the sounds of a fiddle coming up the stairs and realized this wing was over the kitchen and sunroom downstairs.

I peeked through the drapes covering a large window at the end of the hall and looked down on the backyard beyond the carport to a long garage where sat my car and two others of uncertain vintage. Collie's car was not there. The back yard was well lighted against the blackness of the night.

I was restless and didn't want to go right back to my room and I didn't think anyone would mind my looking at the other rooms off the hallway, so I turned from the window and opened the first door on my right. I reached in and felt for a light switch before going in.

This room had been restored as a nursery/ schoolroom, beautifully restored with a cradle and tiny four-poster bed both covered in white organdy ruffles. The carpet had a pastel floral pattern and the walls were pale blue. The other furniture was small and colorful and over the fireplace hung a large painting of a pair of yellow kittens playing with a blue ball. I was really impressed and stood in the middle of the room turning round and round drinking in the beauty. Bottom stayed in the doorway, head cocked to one side probably wondering to whom I was talking as I exclaimed over the details.

Finally I backed out of that lovely room, obviously never lived in, turned off the light, and pulled the door shut. Back in the hall I could again hear the television sounds floating up the back stairway. My soft slippers made no noise as I moved on to another room.

I knew that the other door on the right hand side of the hall had to go into Miss Lucy's room, so I crossed over and tried the first door on my left. It was locked. I went on to the second door which was not locked.

After the nineteenth century charm of the nursery, I was totally unprepared for the sight before me when I turned on the light in this room: Here was the most garishly modern suite of rooms I had ever seen. The ceiling had been lowered from the lofty sixteen feet in the rest of the house to about ten feet, and I was faced with a nightmare of hot pink, purple and a vile shade of green, with many black accents. My first reaction was of pain, as if someone had kicked me in the stomach. Not that I am opposed to modern trends, but this was almost a caricature. The furniture was odd-shaped and uncomfortable looking with much glass and chrome.

I had entered a sitting room and it opened onto a bedroom (the room with the locked door) dominated by a huge bed covered with a spread in a leopard skin pattern with only two or three pieces of black furniture against black walls with hideous orange curtains at the two windows. In fact, the suite had a distinctly masculine tone to it, and my heart sank at the thought that Collie must have decorated these rooms and left the rest of the decorating to his wife.

There was something in these rooms that was like a cruel coldness and Bottom must have felt it too. He had followed me into the suite but did not venture away from my side. We turned from the door of the bedroom to cross the sitting room and leave, Bottom almost leaning against me as we walked.

All of a sudden the lights in the suite went out, leaving us in darkness except for the thin shaft of light where I had left the hall door slightly open.

I gasped and Bottom growled softly. Then we heard the ghost voices.

I knelt beside the dog and put my good arm around him. This time he seemed aware of the voices although the night before he had given no sign that he heard them. There was a difference in the quality of the sounds as if they were muffled and in the distance, and I remembered Collie's explanation of the old ventilating system. If this were the case, then the lowered ceiling would affect the volume. However, as the singing/moaning sounds rose and fell in almost a tune, the logical explanation did not slow down my rapid heartbeat nor my shivering.

In a few moments my eyes became adjusted to the darkness and I stood and started moving slowly over toward the sliver of light at the door, keeping my hand on Bottom's head as he moved right along with me.

Just as we were within three or four feet of the door, it eased shut leaving us in total darkness as the voices seemed to grow louder and to take on an insistent quality. I plunged forward, grabbing at the door, but missed it and clutched at the wall just to the right where the light switch was. There were two switches and my groping hand pushed at both of them.

The lights suddenly came back on and at the same time the ghost voices were drowned out by some sort of raucous music. I leaned against the wall, breathing deeply and trying to calm the pounding in my chest and head. Obviously the second switch activated a sound system. I turned off that switch and the music stopped, giving way to the ghost singing which continued although the lights were still shining. I turned the switch on again and could not hear the singing at all.

I did not even look back around at the two rooms but opened the door and let Bottom walk out ahead of me, then turned off both switches and shut the door behind me.

I decided that I had done enough exploring for one night and rushed around the passageway to my room where Bottom was standing by the door. After we entered, I leaned against the closed door and drew several deep breaths, completely worn out and trying to fight down a wave of nausea. I lost the battle and ran for the bathroom.

I felt better afterwards, but I also felt that I

absolutely had to have some fresh air, so I went over to the French doors and stepped out onto the small balcony with Bottom at my heels as usual.

The chilly air felt good on my flushed face, but I drew the heavy bathrobe closer as a brisk little wind whipped through the elm trees and hurled itself against the house.

While not as brightly lighted as the back yard, the front of the house was lighted by several ornamental lamps on poles. On the left I could see the carriage house, a two-storied affair with lights showing upstairs and down. I assumed that Collie was there grading papers or preparing a lecture since he had said he would be busy until around nine. It was eight-thirty and I didn't know whether I was looking forward to seeing him in thirty minutes or dreading it.

Down the hill on the right I could see the stained glass windows of the little church shining bravely in the blackness. The Wednesday night prayer meeting was breaking up and I could see car lights coming on and hear motors cranking up as the people left. In the stillness, a faint tinkle of laughter floated up the hill and a child called out shrilly for its mama. I smiled, remembering how David and I would go to prayer meeting on Wednesdays with Aunt Ellen at her small country church every summer and how we would stay very close to her when the service was over for fear we might lose her in the darkness outside that little wooden building.

All of a sudden my head cleared and my heart jumped. It was Wednesday night. And I had heard the singing ghosts. But David had assured me that the ghosts did not sing on Wednesday nights. And he had mentioned our long-ago Wednesday nights in that cryptic postcard of his. Could there be some connection between the singing ghosts and the church next door?

All sorts of questions started to rumble around my brain but very quickly disappeared when Bottom started wagging his tail so vigorously that it was beating against my legs. He was looking toward the church side of the house. As I looked over that way, I saw a figure detach itself from the shadows and run nimbly toward the darkness near the house. I could tell that it was Collie and that he had come from the direction of the church. He was passing right under our balcony and Bottom whined a greeting.

"Are you there, Anne?" Collie whispered.

"Yes," I whispered in answer, "but why are we whispering?"

He didn't bother to answer my question. Instead he hissed an order for Bottom and me to go inside immediately. I glanced back toward the church and saw that all the lights inside were out now but there was still an outside light shining brightly in the front and the high steeple was aglow.

As I turned to follow Collie's urgent command, I saw a small light bobbing along behind the church. I rushed in and turned off the one lamp burning in my room and went back to peek out, but the bobbing light was gone.

I was leaning as far out onto the balcony as I could without actually stepping out there, in deference to Collie's insistence that I go in, when I heard the door of my room open and his voice call my name softly. And at that moment I saw the little light behind the church again.

"I'm over here behind the curtains," I said softly and he joined me at once.

"What do you see?" He stepped out onto the balcony and in the muted shadows out there I could tell he was wearing the black outfit I had heard about.

"It looks like somebody with a flashlight is wandering around in the churchyard." I went back out to stand beside him.

"Yes, I see it," he said as the small light bobbed jerkily away from the church and then stopped and then went out again. "I just can't figure out where he goes back there," he stated angrily.

"Who?" I asked.

"Billy Ray Johnson," he hissed. "Wait! There

it is again!" The light appeared just where it had gone off and now it was going back toward the church rapidly and less jerkily than before. "He must have been carrying something before and now doesn't have it."

In a moment the steeple light went out. The elm trees were rustling in the breeze and in the far distance a dog barked. A car engine roared to life and screeched off down the road toward Blue Valley. "Well," said Collie, "there goes the reverend."

He opened the door and led me back into the room, leaving me by the door while he went over to turn on a lamp. All of a sudden Bottom yelped out on the balcony. We had not given him time to follow us in and he was resenting that. I jumped, my nerves about hopelessly frayed, and opened the door to let him rush in.

"You had better go to bed right now," said the professor.

I looked at him in those black clothes and found it easy to believe all the suspicions that kept cropping up in my confused brain and all of the things the others had told me about this dark brooding man. And on top of everything else, the memory of the feelings that I had while standing in that suite of rooms around the corner of the hall made me shudder. But here he was being solicitous of my health.

Or was he just trying to get me safely to bed so he could continue with whatever he had begun before I saw him outside?

There were many questions I would have liked to ask him but I was afraid to speak out. I couldn't ask him anything about Billy Ray Johnson without revealing that Billy Ray had been in this very rocm to warn me about him. And I certainly did not want to risk losing Billy Ray's help should I need it later. I suspected that one of these men could lead me to David and I felt both of them knew more about his disappearance than they were willing to tell me. So I decided the only thing for me to do at the moment was to keep both of them on my side.

"Yes," I said finally. "Perhaps I should go to bed."

There was something in my voice that made him look at me sharply and he drew back the hand he had held out to me when he saw I was making no effort to move closer to him.

"Well, good night then," he said. At the door he turned around and, avoiding my eyes, added, "Please don't tell the old girls that I was up here tonight. I slipped in without their seeing me." And he was gone before I could agree to do as he asked or even say good night to him.

"I'm just too tired to try to think about any of this tonight," I said to myself. Bottom must have agreed, because he went over and crawled under the head of my bed and stretched out with a long sigh.

So I drew a full tub of hot water and, holding my cast up as high as I could, lay in the wonderful warmth and soaked until my aching body relaxed and my brain turned off.

After my bath I found a flannel nightgown that I had brought with me with sleeves large enough to accommodate my cast, put it on, and crawled under the covers. I closed my eyes and told myself to go to sleep.

Chapter Four

Eight hours later I woke up alert and ready to think.
It was five-thirty in the morning, too early to get up
and stir around, so I sat up in bed, wrapped the
bathrobe around my shoulders and piled the pillows
against the headboard so I could lean back and try to
straighten out the thoughts that I had been too tired
to do anything about the night before. There was no
light outside yet, but I could hear the birds chatter-
ing and an occasional rooster crowing far away.
Again I remembered the summers on Aunt Ellen's
farm and how David and I each used to try to wake
up before the other so we could be the first to hear
the rooster crowing and run quietly downstairs to be
alone with Aunt Ellen while she did her morning
chores. I smiled remembering how disgusted the
one was who overslept and missed standing in the
magical mistiness of the chicken yard helping Aunt
Ellen feed her chickens or missed being the one she

sent to the strawberry patch to gather dew-covered berries to go with the oatmeal and biscuits at breakfast. Some mornings we both woke up and other mornings we both overslept, much to our disappointment in both cases. For we were jealous of that time with Aunt Ellen.

But I didn't wake up to think about long ago, I told myself and drew in a quick breath. Or did I? David must have known that if I came to Goldengrove I would remember those childhood days. And was his cryptic postcard message a plea for me to come to Blue Valley? Was his telling me that the ghosts don't sing on Wednesday night connected? What was he trying to tell me? Back then, the only nights we did anything except chase lightning bugs for a few minutes before eight o'clock bedtime was on Wednesday nights when Aunt Ellen took us to prayer meeting.

Why all the concern with Wednesday night? I thought back again to those days with Aunt Ellen and remembered that a big game with us was to say the opposite of what we meant. If one of us said to the other that we didn't want any ice cream, it was a signal to separate and meet a few minutes later at Aunt Ellen's big old refrigerator where she always kept several frozen trays of homemade ice cream left over from Sunday afternoons. We would fill two big spoons with as much cream as they could hold, then smooth over what was left and race out to the back of the house and sit on the grass, leaning against the big oak tree while we licked the sweet coldness. No store-bought ice cream cone ever tasted so good as those stolen scoops. And, of course, Aunt Ellen knew about it all along and would have gladly given us big dishes of the ice cream if we had just asked. But somehow I guess she knew that it tasted better snitched.

So was David telling me that the ghost singing happened on Wednesday nights and that there was something special about that particular night? Surely that was the message, and I felt it included the prayer meeting along with the ghost singing. David had told me that Billy Ray Johnson was going to help him. He knew that I would remember this. Had he been telling me in the last two messages that this minister would help me too? A feeling of relief enveloped me. Surely my brother had been trying to guide me to this red-haired man.

Or had he been trying to warn me against him? Against a minister?

Of course not, I concluded. The thing for me to do was to go over to the parsonage right after breakfast and accept Billy Ray's offer of a ride to town. I could not relax until I had talked with the people at the motel where David had stayed and at the library where I knew he had worked long hours researching the old houses in the area. I tried to put the gnawing doubts about Collie out of mind and to forget the way I felt when he kissed me. Everyone seemed to have some reservations about the professor, even his own cousin and her companion, although I had to admit that Miss Lucy seemed to waver in her condemnation of him. The only person who seemed to accept him as a good fellow all the way was Doc Perkins. And even he had suggested that I trust no one completely.

My mind was beginning to cloud up again so I decided to dress before I lost my courage about asking Billy Ray Johnson for help. By now it was nearly seven o'clock and I could hear Miss Lucy stirring in her room. She came through the bathroom and peeked in to check on me.

"Why, Anne," she said when she saw me climbing out of bed, "why in the world are you getting up so early?"

"Good morning, Miss Lucy," I said, smiling at her concern. "I have slept all I can and have stayed in as long as I can." I walked over close to her and said seriously, "I have to try to find David today."

"I know, dear," she said kindly. "I understand just how you feel. You get dressed and come on downstairs and I'll fix you a good hot breakfast."

"Thank you," I said, thinking how my mother had always thought "a good hot breakfast" was the cure for whatever ailed a person.

I dressed in a tweed skirt and a bulky blue turtleneck with sleeves stretchy enough to fit over the cast, plus thick socks and clunky loafers, then went downstairs with Bottom leading the way. I walked out the front door with him and let him run around in the elm grove for a few minutes and decided that I had dressed appropriately for the weather what with the skirt's matching jacket thrown around my shoulders.

While I was waiting for the dog to finish his romp, I saw the professor leave the carriage house and get into his Cadillac. I stepped behind a tree because I didn't want to have to explain to him what I planned to do since I knew he would object to my asking the minister for help. He drove off down the lane and turned in the direction of Blue Valley. Since he had been carrying a briefcase, I gathered that he was going to work. I was glad he did not see me, but something inside insisted on being a little disappointed that he hadn't checked on me before leaving.

Miss Allie was helping Miss Lucy put the "good hot breakfast" on a table in the cheerful kitchen when I went in with Bottom, who hurried at once to a corner where a pan full of dog food was waiting for him.

"Miss Allie," I said, touched at their thoughtfulness, "how can I ever thank you and Miss Lucy?"

She smiled at me and said good morning, but Miss Lucy answered for her. "She doesn't like to wear her hearing aid in the morning—never has liked to talk before breakfast. But as Collie says, could we do less since that limb from one of Goldengrove's trees hurt you so badly."

She poured a cup of coffee for me and told me to sit down and butter my biscuits before they got cold. Then she and Miss Allie sat with me and we ate our meal with Miss Lucy and me chatting a little along the way and Miss Allie enjoying her breakfast in silence, a little smile on her face, seemingly completely unconcerned about anything we might be saying. As I settled back to drink a second cup of coffee, I asked Miss Lucy, "Don't you think I should move out into the motel this morning?"

"Well," she said sighing, "I just don't know."

"Absolutely not!" exclaimed Miss Allie suddenly. And Miss Lucy whispered to me behind her hand that Miss Allie could read lips. "Until you are stronger, you should be here where Lucy and I can look after you."

I decided that it would be foolish to argue with her, and was actually relieved that she wanted me to stay, so I didn't pursue the matter. I was in a hurry to be on my way to Blue Valley anyway, so I ran upstairs to get my purse.

When I went back downstairs, Miss Allie and Miss Lucy were in the back entryway talking with Billy Ray. I was glad to see that Miss Allie had at last put on her hearing aid.

"Good morning, Miss Annie," the good-looking young man said as he saw me coming down the stairway and he limped over to shake hands with me—or rather to hold my hand in his while he looked into my face. "I do believe you look better today," he said and smiled into my eyes. "You ladies are doing right by our Annie."

"Indeed they are," I agreed and slipped my hand from his to go over and join the others. Bottom came in to stand beside me, but he didn't growl at the man this time; neither did the man speak to him. "But what are you doing over here so early?"

"I told you I want to help," he said. "I came over to see what you need me to do." His manner was so sweet and his expression so open that I had to be glad to see him. It was beginning to be hard for me to understand Collie's bitter feelings toward this young minister.

"Well," I told him, "as a matter of fact, I was just leaving to go over to your house to see if you would drive me in to Blue Valley this morning."

"I'll be happy to drive you," he answered. "I have nothing pressing to do until six o'clock tomorrow night for a wedding rehearsal at the church, so my day is yours."

"Oh, I don't want to take up your whole day," I assured him.

"Now, Anne," he said, "don't start talking like that. I want to help you find your brother. After all, he must have been on his way to my house when he disappeared."

Miss Lucy and Miss Allie joined in, insisting that I let him help me all day if necessary, especially since I was a stranger in the area. So with all three urging me, I had to agree. "But you'll have to wait here while I run back and get my car," he said. "I walked over."

"Let's take my car," I suggested.

"Yes, Billy Ray," said Miss Allie, "that might be better since we could just tell Collie that Anne went to town and not mention you."

Miss Lucy nodded. "It would save a lot of explaining."

"Oh," I muttered, "maybe I should just try to drive with one hand."

"Nonsense," all three said at once. And that settled that.

I asked if the two ladies minded my leaving Bottom there since I wasn't sure how long he might have to sit in the car if we took him along, and they assured me that they didn't mind at all. In fact, there was a back screened porch where he would be safe and should be happy while I was gone. Bottom wasn't too sure just how happy he would be when I put him on the porch, but I set a bowl of water out there and threw him some dog biscuits and he forgave me.

We left Goldengrove in my little Fiat, and as we were going down the lane toward the road, Billy Ray seemed to be having difficulty with my car. "I believe I'd rather drive my own car, if you don't mind, Anne," he said. I had forgotten that his lame leg might make it hard to manage a clutch.

"Of course, I don't mind," I answered, "but shouldn't we just leave my car back in the garage and walk over to pick up yours?"

"No," he said, shaking his head. "Let's hide yours behind my house and then Rockford won't be sure that you didn't drive off one-armed by yourself."

Across from the church, he swung up into the driveway of a house I had not even noticed when I drove by before. It was a sprawling comfortable-looking house painted green and sitting in a clump of pine trees. He stopped soon and told me to wait while he put my car up and brought his own around, so I got out and stood admiring the beauty of the little white church and listening to the wind in the pines. Soon the preacher came back in the same large car I had seen on Tuesday afternoon, a new

Chrysler Imperial.

"I must say you people up here in Mississippi drive fine cars," I commented as I crawled in beside him and accepted his help fastening the seat belt. "In New Orleans we aren't used to such luxury as an everyday thing."

He smiled and set the powerful machine into motion on the road. "Well," he said as we took off down the hill, "around here there are so many bad roads to contend with that a small car shakes to pieces before very long. My church members live all over these woods and I have to have a car I can depend on to get me there and back. Besides I do mission work in Birmingham one day a week."

I managed to make small talk most of the way towards Blue Valley, but my stomach was a knot of dread at what I might find once I really started looking for my brother. It was hard to believe that up here in this lovely country of rolling pasture land and multicolored woods David could have just vanished or that anything terrible could have happened to him, but my mind kept shouting, *Where is he? Where do I start looking for him?*

We crossed a little creek where on one bank two women were fishing and on the other side some red cows were drinking. And we drove by a fire tower a man in a red plaid jacket was beginning to climb. There were cotton patches showing white among dead stalks, where silvered cabins sat solemnly while thin shafts of smoke curled out of their chimneys, each house complete with television antenna and front porch.

And then after a fifteen-minute year, we rounded a curve and dipped down a long hill into Blue Valley whose main street ran between a row of stately old houses to the town square which was built around a courthouse designed with the ever popular large white columns.

Billy Ray eased the car into a parking space in front of a bank. "Now," he said as he turned off the engine, "where do we start?"

I looked around the square. "Let me think a minute," I answered.

David had mentioned three places in town and I could see all three of them from where we were sitting. The post office was just down the street from the bank; in the next block stood the public library, and on the far corner across another street was the motel where he had stayed. The town was clean and shining with new paint and bright store fronts as if there had been a general face-lifting process recently. I had the feeling I had been set down in the middle of a stage set for a Deep South play as I watched the people on the streets scurrying through the brisk morning air to begin the town's daily process. It was unreal that I should be here in this Mississippi town watching these strangers and wondering where David was. I would not have been surprised had a villain in frock coat and waxed mustache popped around one of the corners and sneered at me. I shuddered.

"May I make a suggestion?" asked Billy Ray.

"Please do," I answered gratefully. And he suggested I go to the motel first if I thought it would help to talk with the manager there while he went to the police station to see if they had heard anything. I agreed, eager to do anything to get started on my search.

"I'll meet you at the library when I finish at the motel," I told him and he nodded agreement.

I could not see the police station from where we were parked so I assumed it was on the side of the courthouse hidden from view, and sure enough, Billy Ray started off in the opposite direction I had to take to reach the motel. I hurried around the square and went into the motel lobby.

A little old lady with obviously dyed short red hair was behind a counter reading the morning paper. A half-empty coffee cup sat at her elbow and a fat orange cat was lying farther down the counter eyeing the cup.

"Good morning," I said, and the old woman and the cat both looked up at me.

"Well, I don't know about that," said she, "my

rheumatism has been hurting me this morning."
And then she smiled, which made her wrinkled face
seem not so old after all. "Can I help you?"

I took a deep breath. "My name is Anne
Whitehead and I'm looking for my brother David
who was registered here until last week."

She laughed. "I thought you looked familiar.
You look just like him." And then she turned serious. "Do you have any identification on you?"

I was surprised but opened my purse and pulled
out my wallet. "Of course," I said. "Will you look
in my wallet at my driver's license?"

She looked at the outstretched wallet and then
my broken arm and cautiously reached out.

"Why do you ask for my identification?" I
asked.

"Miss Whitehead," she said, "I don't know
what your brother is mixed up in but I like that boy
and he woke me up about two A.M. last Saturday
looking scared and gave me two envelopes. He told
me to let nobody have them except his sister if she
came here and asked me to mail that strange card to
you, too." She checked my wallet and then reached
over to drop it into my purse. I could think of nothing to say.

She continued, "Two men have come in asking
me if David left anything at all here and I've lied for
him because I can't help but think that boy was in

some sort of trouble not of his own doing."

"Did you know the men?"

"No," she shook her head. "But then I'm sort of new to Blue Valley. Came here to run this place for my son while he's in the service. Oh, they came at different times."

She went over to a little safe and returned with two envelopes, one smaller than the other. Before handing them to me she glanced outside. "He told me to give you this one if someone was with you," and she handed me the smaller of the two. "And he said to slip this one to you and not let the person with you see it so you'd best hide it."

"Why?" I asked, looking out. I saw Billy Ray limping toward the building. I looked back at the woman and saw that her face had turned pale.

"That's one of the men came asking about David," she whispered. "Don't show him that big envelope."

I hurriedly stuffed the larger envelope into my purse under a scarf and picked up the smaller one just as Billy Ray came in the door. "Thank you very much," I told the woman who ignored Billy Ray and started batting at her cat who had eased down the counter and was busily lapping up her coffee.

"You found something," he said as we went out, and he reached for the envelope. "Let me help you open this."

"Yes," I answered. "The woman said she thought David must have been in some sort of trouble because he asked her to keep this for me."

"The old hag," Billy Ray muttered under his breath.

"What?" I asked, thinking maybe I had misunderstood him.

He clenched his teeth. "I asked her if David had left anything at all behind and even got her to let me search the room where he stayed."

"But, Billy Ray," I said, "David had left this for me and she wanted to wait to see if I appeared on the scene."

He relaxed a bit. "Yes, I'm sure she was right, Anne, but if it is a lead, I could have been working on it several days sooner if she had just given it to me." He had the envelope open and we found two rolls of exposed film inside

"What do you suppose these are pictures of?" I asked, reaching in and pulling out the film. It was carefully taped with David's name written on the tape.

"Are you sure this was all?" Billy Ray asked, looking at me closely.

I met his stare. "As far as I know," I answered and reached for the envelope. "Let's look inside and see if there is something else there. It does look like he would have left me a note saying what this means." There was nothing else inside the envelope so I started to fold it up to stick it in my pocket, but Billy Ray reached over and took it from me and put it in his own pocket.

"I know a drugstore up the street where we can get this film developed in one day," he said looking down at the two little cylinders. "I'll run down there and put these in and meet you back at the library."

"I think I'll just go with you." I suddenly felt that I should keep my eye on the film. "I need a box of tissues." He didn't argue with me so we walked on around the square past a ten-cent store with windows filled with Halloween jack-o-lanterns to a neat little drugstore with a seed store in a back room. "Did you find out anything at the police station?" I asked as we walked into the store.

"Not a thing," he said and shook his head sadly. He picked up a box of tissues and went over to a clerk.

"Here," I said reaching for my purse, "let me pay for the tissues and I'll pay for the film developing, too."

He smiled at me sweetly. "Not at all," he said. "My treat."

I smiled back and didn't argue because I was really afraid to try to pull out my wallet with my awkward left hand for fear I would dislodge the other envelope. He paid the bill and slipped the receipt for the film into his wallet. "I'll run in and pick these up for you tomorrow," he said.

"Thank you," I said, "but I hate to put you to so much trouble." But I knew that I had lost this round because the wallet was safely back in his pocket.

"No trouble," he assured me, told the clerk good-bye, and led me back out onto the square. He carried my tissues tucked under one arm and manipulated his cane with the other. In spite of his lame leg, there was absolutely nothing weak about this man. I hurried along beside him and tried to evaluate his reaction to the film. He had become downright tense on seeing the envelope, but when he saw its contents, his manner had changed to a cross between disappointment and anger. A small shiver ran down my spine at the memory of the coldness in those blue eyes when he asked me if I was sure there was nothing else David had left. I decided I was being overly sensitive and suspicious.

"I wonder what David took pictures of that he didn't want to carry with him when he left," I mused as we walked toward the library.

"Maybe he found some ghosts to photograph," Billy Ray said wryly.

I stopped. "I'll bet you're right!" I exclaimed. "Maybe he did get some psychic pictures and was afraid he might lose them."

"But how did he know you would come and get

them?" asked Billy Ray lightly as we walked on. "Did he send you a message?"

"Not exactly," I said, "but evidently he knew that he would be out of circulation and that I would be worried." He looked around at me with a strange expression on his face. The shiver again. "I had told him I might run up to see him some time if he stayed up here very long," I lied. And then asked myself why I was lying to this man. Why was it that both of the men who could be of help produced feelings of doubt and fear in me? Surely both of them could not be on the wrong side, but which one could I trust? Neither one, I decided.

"Here we are at the library," stated Billy Ray and started up the steep steps. I followed him slowly, matching my pace to his limpy one. "I have already checked through most of the books David was using to see if there might be a clue there," he said, "but I know you'll feel better if you look through them yourself."

"Oh," I said, "David told me that he met you in the library. Do you come here often?"

"Fairly often," he said as we reached the top of the steps. "I don't have too much to do in my spare time around here except read."

"Then you can show me where to look for the books David was using," I said and preceded him into the building which looked and smelled like every other small library I had ever entered. And there was the same polite lady librarian behind the work counter pasting new checkout slips into old books. She smiled at us as we walked by, Billy Ray stopping to ask how her mother was feeling that morning. I wandered on but he called me back and introduced us, and she too exclaimed over my looking like the Mr. Whitehead who had been working so hard in her library during the past few weeks. I was polite, as polite as I could be while feeling that everywhere I turned something was trying to slow me down in my search for David.

The envelope in my purse was worrying me—it was a heavy brown envelope and when I put it in my purse, I could feel that there was a small box inside. All the way to the library from the motel I had been trying to figure out, without looking preoccupied, just what it could be. There was a small tape recorder on the long table behind the librarian's counter and all of a sudden I knew that what I had in that envelope in my purse was a tape box. David did most of his note taking with a tape recorder. Of course, it must be a tape of something incriminating to somebody. And I did not dare open my purse to feel the envelope again. Nor did I dare go to the restroom right then because as surely as I did, Billy Ray would suspect that the motel woman had given me something else. So all I could do for the present was to see what else I could find.

Billy Ray led me to a far corner of the reading room where a whole section of shelving was devoted to antebellum homes.

"I think I know all of the books that list Blue Valley homes," he said quietly, pulling at least ten books down and carrying them to a nearby study table.

I looked at the pile of books and my heart sank: more delay. Then I had a thought. "Since you have already looked through them all," I said, "why don't I just go through the ones that mention Goldengrove in detail and see if I get any ideas."

He nodded and went through the volumes, pulling out three of them. Two of the books were picture stories of various old homes and Goldengrove received its due, even to a picture of it in the fall with the elm trees showing as a truly golden grove. But the third volume was a collection of stories on the haunted houses of the Deep South. New Orleans had its share of the limelight and one or two houses over in Alabama were discussed, but Goldengrove's singing ghosts took up an entire chapter.

"Oh, look, Billy Ray," I said on finding the story.

"Yes," he said, "I've read it."

I sat down at the table but he remained standing. "I think I'll run an errand or two while you read all this, Anne."

"All right. Where do you want me to meet you."

"At the car? In about thirty minutes?"

I agreed and eagerly settled down to read the tale of the ghosts I had heard twice. It seems that the legend of the singing ghosts dates back to the very beginnings of Goldengrove when the huge house was built over an unmarked burial place for the slaves of the man who had sold the land to the professor's ancestors. The man was something of a maniac who was alternately very good and very brutal to his slaves, and this was supposed to explain the fact that sometimes the ghosts sang happy songs and sometimes sad, melancholy ones.

There was even the story of how on the site of the magnificent place, there had originally stood a grove of elm trees which nearby residents insisted was haunted, where there was always a cold wind and the eerie howling of the spirits of the slaves buried among the trees. In a letter dated a few years after he built the mansion, the first owner was quoted as saying that the man who sold him the property neglected to inform him that the burial grounds existed. He also wrote that, although the house was obviously haunted (especially in the fall of the year), he and his family were not afraid of the ghosts.

The house was built originally with several secret passages (that seem to have been boarded up) and a ventilating system, which some people use to explain the ghostly sounds. The current owner blocked some of the ventilating system and did extensive renovation of the mansion which cut down considerably on the volume of the singing and the frequency of times it is heard. (Marley's efforts in the upstairs rooms.) There was also the story told of how the ghosts have always been fond of the masters of Goldengrove and watchful of the women they loved. As long as the owner loved the lady of the house and she was faithful to him, the ghosts sang happy songs; but if he stopped loving her or she was unfaithful to him, the songs turned sad.

How exciting this must have seemed to David! And how happy for him that he had decided to visit Goldengrove in the fall. I hoped he had indeed heard the ghost voices.

Before he left, Billy Ray replaced all the books except the three I had wanted to check, so I put those three on a book cart and went back to speak to the librarian.

"Thank you very much," I said.

"Did you find what you were looking for?" she asked in that quiet voice librarians seem to have from birth.

"I was just trying to find out what my brother

had done in here in the way of research," I answered.

"Are you interested in ghosts also, Miss Whitehead?"

"Only to be able to talk with my brother about the matter," I said smiling, suddenly deciding that I didn't want to talk with this woman after all. I couldn't tell her that David had disappeared just as I hadn't told the motel woman that he was gone. So I nodded goodbye to her and left, finding the cool air outside refreshing after the musty warmth of the library.

I stood on the steps a moment to breathe in some of the fresh air before walking back to where Billy Ray had parked his car.

He was sitting in it, and I had the feeling that he was ready to leave so I hated to suggest looking around further. Also, I could use his wanting to leave as an excuse to get back to Goldengrove and try to find a tape recorder.

"Ready to go?" he asked as I got in. He had opened the door for me from the inside.

"Well…" I hesitated, sliding into the plush seat.

"What is it?"

"The only other place I know of to look is in the parking lots to see if I can find David's car. Surely it couldn't have just disappeared."

He turned to face me. "Anne, I have checked

every parking lot in town and none of them had his car in it."

I let my features droop visibly in disappointment but deep down I didn't believe he had checked those lots at all. I felt he wanted me to get out of Blue Valley. However my droopy feelings were convincing.

"Don't worry, honey," he said patting my free hand.

"Let's take all this to mean David drove his car off somewhere to do some checking on his ghosts and will show up soon." I smiled faintly at him and he started the car. "It's eleven-thirty, almost time to eat," he said. "Do you want to eat in town or go back to the country?"

He reached around behind me and drew me nearer and took my hand away from my eyes. "We found the film, Anne," he reassured me.

"Yes," I said, feeling way down in the dumps. "But we have to wait till tomorrow to see the pictures."

"What you need is something to eat," he declared and pulled out of the parking space. "I know just the place to get a fine steak lunch a few miles out of town."

As we drove off, I saw a little old man peering at us through a window in the bank. It cheered me up somewhat. "We'd better go somewhere," I laughed. "That banker is wondering who your new girl is, Brother Johnson."

"Let him wonder," he chuckled and raced off up the street.

I couldn't possibly feel the morning had been a loss because at the motel I had found the film and the other thing in my purse which had to be a tape. And at the library I had learned the story of the ghosts of Goldengrove. And at the post office—

"We forgot the post office," I said with disgust in my voice.

"Don't worry," answered Billy Ray, coming to a stop at the intersection of a wide highway. "We'll go back into town after lunch. I have another errand to do then anyway." His strong freckled hands guided the big car out onto the highway and we began to pick up speed.

I kept track of the direction we had taken, the nagging apprehension of this man still bothering me. I tried to shake off this feeling by telling myself that he was a minister and the only thing on which I was basing my suspicion was Collie's hatred of the man. Unless. Unless David had tried with his insistent repetition of the word Wednesday and his reminding me of our summer-nights prayer meetings to tell me something about the preacher. And then there was Bottom's reaction to the man.

But there was the trust the little old ladies at

Goldengrove had in him. Had he cleverly managed to convince them that Collie was evil in order to carry on some evil scheme of his own? In spite of the fact that I had tried to accept the idea that something was not quite on the up and up as far as Collie was concerned, I could not help regretting that I had set out on this day with Billy Ray.

As I watched the outskirts of town turn into pasture land, I decided perhaps I might learn a few things from this man beside me without letting him know I was apprehensive.

Neither of us had spoken since turning onto the highway until I said in a confidential way, "I heard the ghosts singing last night."

He glanced at me quickly. "Oh?"

"Please don't tell anybody because I didn't say anything about it at Goldengrove." Maybe if he thought he had my confidence, he would say something to confirm my suspicions of him.

"I won't," he promised and smiled. "Were you frightened?"

"You don't believe in the ghosts?" I asked.

"I didn't say that," he said. "I've heard them too. Or at least I've heard the sounds people attribute to the ghosts. But you didn't answer my question—were you afraid of them?"

"Well, it wasn't the most pleasant experience I've had, but I don't think I was all that frightened,"

I said and then went on to tell him where I was when I heard the singing, without expressing my horror on seeing the suite.

He laughed. "You were in Marley's apartment. Isn't that a fantastic pair of rooms?"

"At least," I said dryly. "So that was where the Andrews lived?"

"No, not the Andrews, just Marley," he said, pulling off the road to stop at a small Texaco service station. "Rockford gave her those rooms to decorate as she pleased. He did the rest of the house. You can see how they could never have gotten along."

I could indeed, and my heart gave a little jump for joy.

The service station attendant came up, and Billy Ray asked him to fill the gas tank with premium.

I saw my chance to look in the envelope, so I said that I thought I would powder my nose before lunch and got out. On the way to the restroom, I noticed that there was a public telephone booth inside the station and decided I should call Goldengrove and tell Miss Lucy not to expect me for lunch. As I started toward the booth, Billy Ray jumped out of the car and in spite of that crippled leg reached the booth just as I did.

I told him what I was about to do and asked him sweetly to dial the number for me since he probably already knew it and because of my hurt arm. I don't think he really wanted to dial that number, but there were two or three other people standing around and there was nothing else he could do. He dialed a number and waited for an answer. I held out my hand for the phone but he was reluctant to give it up until he himself had spoken with Miss Lucy who answered at Goldengrove.

For a moment I was afraid he had dialed another number and that I would not be allowed to talk, but after listening carefully for a moment and saying a few "yes ma'ams" he handed it over. I said hello to her and she started babbling about how we must rush on home at once because Dr. Perkins had dropped by just that moment and would wait for us to return so he could check my injuries. It seemed he was worried about my headache. She had plenty of lunch for me and we should not take time to eat before coming back. If we hurried we could be there before the professor, who had called to say he couldn't leave the campus until twelve-thirty.

I didn't know how far we were from Goldengrove, but I assured her that I would see to it that we came in as soon as possible. I hung up and told Billy Ray I was sorry about not being able to eat that steak lunch. I decided not to go to the restroom after all and returned to the car while he paid the bill.

As I sat there in Billy Ray's car, something

seemed to tell me that I should move David's envelope out of my purse, so I took it out and stuck it
inside the sling where I held it tightly against my
body with my upper arm. I had it well hidden and
securely placed by the time Billy Ray came back to
the car.

He entered the automobile as usual by sitting
down and swinging both legs together around under
the wheel and then putting the cane on the floor
under his legs. I noticed not for the first time that
morning the fine quality of the suit he was wearing—a rusty-colored tweed just right for the weather—and tried to hide the relief in my voice when I
said again that I was sorry to have to change his
plans for lunch.

Without saying a word, he reached over me and
picked up my purse from the floorboard beside my
right foot and set it down on the seat between us.
My heart picked up speed but I was determined that
he wouldn't see much reaction from me.

I gave a little laugh and asked, "Won't that be in
your way there?"

"Not at all," he said, opening the large leather
bag. "I thought I would help you take the shine off
your nose before we go in." He rummaged around
in the roomy depths and took out the scarf. He
shook it and reached back in for my cosmetics bag.

"Here, I can do it," I said and reached over for

the little flowered pouch, but he held it back and opened it, then pulled out my compact and a comb. He held up the tiny mirror for me while I patted the powder over my nose and cheeks and then gave me the comb to run through my hair. I could see that his other hand was feeling around inside the purse, and I was glad that I did not have to perform any other reparation acts because my hand had begun to tremble.

"Is that better?" I asked lightly, putting the comb back inside the cosmetics bag as he dropped in the compact.

"Much," he said just as lightly and started the engine. I picked up the purse and dropped it over where it had been and held up my seat belt for him to fasten. "We'll be there in ten minutes," he added. "I know a shortcut."

And he did. Or at least he knew how to fly over the road he took because we were at Goldengrove in about eight minutes, neither of us having spoken during that time. The radio was on so we had an accompaniment of country music along the woodsy road which ended at an intersection with the road toward the Crossroads just about half a mile from Goldengrove. He stopped at the gate and told me to wait while he fetched my car. That way I would just have the lane to maneuver with my one good arm. Then he left in a swirl of dust and was back in a few minutes with my Fiat.

He held the door for me and then leaned in the window. "I'll be in touch," he said and kissed me lightly on the lips.

I thanked him for taking me to town and sped up the lane feeling as though I needed to wash out my mouth. With soap.

But a stronger feeling gripped me as I neared the house: a feeling of happiness that I was back at Goldengrove.

Chapter Five

Breathing a sigh of relief, I gathered up my purse and the box of tissues Billy Ray had bought. The car door flew open before I could reach for the handle, and Collie was leaning in to pull me out. His car was parked on the other side of the two vehicles I had seen from the hall window, and under the carport there was another car which I assumed belonged to Doc Perkins.

I was thoroughly exhausted and felt that I would fall apart if I couldn't soon find a place to be alone to open the envelope clutched to my side. I'm afraid I turned a face full of exasperation toward the professor as I stood up beside him. Whatever I felt could have been as nothing, however, compared to the angry concern in his face. He glared down at me and the hands on my arms were rough.

"What do you mean going off with that man?"

he snarled, his fingers digging into my upper arms.

I was too tired to be polite. "Let me alone, Professor," I snapped back, avoiding his eyes. "You know I have to look for David and I have trouble driving with one hand."

"You could have waited for me to drive you."

"I had waited longer than I should have already."

"Look at me," he ordered.

I reluctantly removed my gaze from the rafters and met his burning black eyes. I had been avoiding those eyes because I had already found that when we were standing close, whatever good resolves I made to avoid putting my complete trust in this man seemed to fly away to be replaced by a desire to trust him more than completely.

"All right," I said nastily.

He looked as though I had slapped him. His grip on my arms loosened and he seemed to change his mind about what he wanted to say. "Doc Perkins is waiting for you," he said finally.

"Then he really is here?" I asked. "I thought this was just a way to get me back here and away from Billy Ray." I walked out of the garage. He let me get a few feet away and called my name softly. I stopped but didn't turn around to face him again.

"I was worried about you," he said, "so I made Miss Lucy tell me where you were. Then when you called in, I thought it was a good time to bring you back." His voice changed to a fierce whisper. "Can't you understand that I'm afraid you might be in the same kind of danger David fell into?"

I had not thought of it in that light at all. I turned slowly and faced him. "Then you knew that David was in danger?"

"I suspected it when I saw him Saturday in the post office," he said shortly. "He had a frightened air about him and wouldn't stop to talk with me at all."

"I think we may have made some progress this morning," I told him. He walked out of the garage and we started moving toward the house. I was just going to tell him about the film when Miss Allie came to the back door and called to us to hurry because the doctor was becoming impatient.

"I want to hear everything that happened this morning," he said. "As soon as you see the doctor and eat your lunch, meet me out here."

I agreed and rushed on into the sunroom where Doc Perkins was waiting with the two old ladies. I was touched that the old doctor would come so far to check on me, a new patient and a stranger in the community, but he insisted that he had had other things to do in the neighborhood and was anxious to check my wounds.

As Dr. Perkins started to reach for my broken

arm, I realized that I couldn't let him mess around with that arm without revealing the envelope still inside the sling so I hastily excused myself and asked him to wait while I ran upstairs to the bathroom. The doctor had an annoyed expression on his sweet old face and it did not match his usual sunny disposition. Even though I thought that he probably had waited for me all he felt he could, I had to get rid of the envelope without letting anyone see it, so I sped up the back stairway before anyone could object. I called back as I left the room that I would be right back and didn't wait for one of the three older people to answer.

At the top of the back stairway I wished I had gone up the front way instead because a cold feeling hit me as I stepped into the hallway that ran by the grotesque apartment where I had heard the ghostly singing. I hadn't realized before how much I depended on Bottom for company and protection in this monstrous house. In order to avoid making noise on the uncarpeted floor as I went past those rooms, I took off my shoes, left them beside the top of the stairs, and ran lightly down the hall and around the corner to my room.

In spite of the fact that the doctor was impatient to examine me, I could not resist looking inside the envelope so I rushed into the bathroom and locked both doors. Then I sat down on the edge of the tub and pulled out the sealed envelope. I turned on the water in the lavatory before rattling the paper to open the seal. Inside I found, as I had suspected, a small box containing a roll of recording tape. The white leader tape on the roll was marked in David's handwriting:

GHOSTS AND OTHER NOISES
AT GOLDENGROVE

There was no note, no writing on the box, nothing except the few words on the leader tape. And me with no tape recorder. And with a tape that David obviously didn't want anyone but me to hear. A tape that I had to hide carefully in a hurry.

I was still clutching the drugstore bag with the box of tissues under my good arm. I laid it on the lavatory while I paced around the big old-fashioned bathroom trying to think of a place to hide the envelope and the tape box. I didn't dare put the envelope in the wastebasket because of the definite shape of the tape box marked on it in wrinkles from being clutched so tightly against my body.

The tissue box. I hastily opened the slit on top and removed a stack of tissues half as thick as the tape box. I folded the stack in two and stuffed it into one end of the envelope, pushing the tape box down to the other end. Then I lifted out about half of the rest of the tissues and put the envelope, which was almost exactly the same length as the tissue box was wide, into the box and carefully pushed the rest of the tissues back into the box and set it over on the back of the commode.

All of this had taken only a few minutes, but I felt as though an eternity had passed as I raced back along the hallway to slip on my shoes and run down the stairs.

"Here she is," said Doc Perkins as I entered the sunroom. "You're giving me more of a noontime rest than I usually get, young lady." He laughed good-naturedly but I felt he was really a bit upset with me for detaining.him. But, after all, I thought to myself, I hadn't asked him to come by.

I couldn't help wondering if he paid this much attention to all his patients. In fact, I was a bit annoyed myself at having to slow down again in my effort to find David when I could have been trying to find a tape recorder or telling Collie what had happened in town. But this feeling made me ashamed of myself when the doctor was willing to take up his time to check on me, so I smiled and took my jacket from around my shoulders and the arm from the sling and held the cast out for him to check for whatever doctors check for with broken arms. He seemed more interested in my head, however, and asked several questions about headaches and blurry vision. He seemed satisfied with my answers and started to leave soon after warning me to be careful about getting too tired. I couldn't agree to take the nap he tried to insist upon, but I did promise to eat a sandwich and to run around very little.

Before going out the door, the good doctor set down his bag and picked up my jacket from the couch where I had thrown it, commented on the softness of the material while holding it folded up in his arms, then gently laid it back around my shoulders with some comment on how I shouldn't get chilled.

Chilled in this warm room? My head reeled and my lungs felt as though someone had pushed all the air from them: Kind old Doc Perkins had been searching my jacket. But it was as impossible to believe that he could be mixed up in David's disappearance as it was to believe that a minister could be—or a professor either for that matter.

Miss Lucy was leading me into the kitchen where she had put out the sandwich I had promised to eat along with some of her ever-present and delicious iced tea. I thought I might choke if I ate the food, but it was eat or fight this determined woman.

Miss Allie had turned on the television in the sunroom and was settling down to watch her afternoon soap operas, and outside I could hear the doctor start his car engine and drive off down the lane. Everything seemed to move in slow motion and the only thing I knew to do to set things back at a normal speed was to go ahead and eat the food as quickly as possible.

Miss Lucy insisted that I didn't look strong enough to do anything else that day, and I took a long drink of the sweet iced tea, hoping it would make me feel stronger. I didn't want to talk with her, so I kept eating and hoping she wouldn't ask me a question.

Luckily, Collie must have grown tired of waiting for me outside because he came across the yard and into the back door asking as he entered the kitchen if the doctor found me healthy. I nodded and took another bite as Miss Lucy began telling him how the doctor had insisted I rest and how I was refusing to listen to his advice.

Collie came over to the table as she turned back to the sink where she was washing dishes and he sat down across from me. I turned stricken eyes to his face, this time seeking understanding. He looked puzzled but somehow caught the message that I needed to get away from there and talk to him.

"Hurry and finish that sandwich and let's take Bottom for a short run," he said. "That should relax you as much as taking a nap and then you can go back to searching for your brother."

My gratitude was plain for him to see and I forced down the rest of the sandwich and thanked

Miss Lucy while he went over to the back porch and let Bottom rush in. The good old dog was overjoyed to see me and I hastened to get him out of the kitchen before he wrecked it in his exuberance.

Collie led Bottom and me out behind the garage and down the hill a bit to a place where a brick barbecue grill and a picnic table with benches stood near a little creek. All of the trees in the area had been cleared away except for one majestic old oak which must have seen many generations of children playing in the clear water of the shallow stream beneath it.

I sat down at the table, but Collie wandered about until he found a stick to throw for Bottom to fetch. He was deliberately letting me pull together my thoughts, but I found it a little difficult to do so in this quiet place when my thoughts were so far from quiet.

Birds were chirping in the oak and far overhead an airplane droned along, while nearby the dead leaves made scratchy sounds as the professor romped with my dog. The leaves directly under the tree were still a bit soggy from all the rain, but where the dog was running, the sun had dried them out and occasionally Bottom would get sidetracked from chasing the stick into snapping at the leaves that were flying under his feet.

But I knew that I could not let this idyllic scene

keep me from trying to determine what everything I had seen and heard meant as far as my brother was concerned. Quite obviously there was more than met the eye going on around Goldengrove and the little church next door. But what could it be? And just who was mixed up in it? I was sure that Billy Ray Johnson knew more than he should about the situation but I could not decide if the professor was in reality a partner with the preacher in whatever was going on or just what was going on there.

And now I had to suspect the doctor. Surely I had not imagined his feeling my coat pockets, and neither had I imagined Billy Ray searching my purse. Had Collie searched my car while I was seeing the doctor? Were they all involved together? And in what?

And the ghost voices. There was a distinct difference between the sounds I had heard the first time and the sounds I heard in the dead woman's wild rooms. The lowered ceiling could account for the muffled tone, but as I thought back to the first night when Bottom and I were crouched behind the drapes in my room, it seemed that the sounds I heard then had an almost artificial ring to them. Was this somebody trying to scare me off? The fact that Bottom had paid no attention to the singing that night seemed significant and the fact he had been obviously affected by the second singing even more sig-

nificant. If the first time had been a recording someone had managed to pipe into the lovely golden
room, then Bottom would have thought nothing
about it because he was accustomed to hearing all
sorts of music and sound effects on our music
machines at home. And thinking back to the first
night when I had been hurt and groggy I realized I
hadn't paid too much attention to the fact that the
bathroom door which Miss Lucy was sure she had
left open had been closed at some point. I could
remember now that my door had been ajar while I
was lying in bed watching the lightning show up the
various parts of the room. So someone with a tape
player could have come in.

But why? To scare me off, obviously. But on
the other hand, if someone had been in the room,
wouldn't Bottom have been concerned? Not when
he was behind those thick drapes and already concerned about the storm. Then if the singing in my
room had been human and not ghostly, the sounds I
heard in the other rooms must have been the real
ghosts. I shivered out there in the peaceful outdoors
remembering the chill and darkness in Marley's
rooms with the eerie wailing over my head.

But whatever was going on in that house had to
extend beyond those rooms and that eerie wailing.
Could it be connected with the death of Collie's
wife? And if it was, then was David's life in dan-

ger? My heart sank at the further thought that he might already be dead.

While I sat there at a picnic table thinking about ghosts, I started to get up and suggest we leave, but at that point Collie came over and sat down opposite me, leaving Bottom to play by himself. At first the big dog didn't like that idea and ran up to put his stick on the bench beside Collie, barking for it to be thrown, but finally he realized that the game was over and contented himself with getting a noisy drink from the stream.

"Do you feel better now?" Collie asked.

"Not much," I admitted. "I have too many things running around in my mind that I can't put together."

He slipped off his jacket and laid it across the other end of the table. I looked at it a moment, admiring the red lining showing under the navy wool. David had a jacket similar to that one.

"I don't want to push you," he said then, "but tell me just what happened this morning and what you found."

"Well, when we arrived in Blue Valley," I began, but he interrupted.

"No," he said, "start at the very beginning. With how you got in touch with the preacher in the first place." His jaw was set and his eyes intense, so I found myself telling him about the first two times

I had heard or seen Billy Ray at Goldengrove as well as the fact that he was there offering to drive me before I had a chance to ask him.

As I told about hearing the conversation outside my door while I was supposedly asleep, Collie picked up Bottom's stick and carefully broke it into many little pieces which he pushed around into various designs while he listened, commenting on my tale only in short grunts of exclamation once in a while. I didn't leave out the things Billy Ray said about Collie and as I talked, he would lift his eyes from the stick pieces occasionally to meet mine. I paused at the end of that part of my story and he muttered, "And do you believe all you heard?"

I quite honestly said, "I don't know what to believe."

His shoulders drooped slightly. And I couldn't help blurting out a question that had been bothering me no end. "What were you doing stalking around in the night in that black outfit?"

He looked up. "Would you believe that last night I was looking for David?"

I was amazed. "In the yard at Goldengrove?"

"Please don't ask me right now where I had been," he begged. "Just trust me."

"Doc Perkins told me not to trust anybody completely," I said and then blanched thinking about the good doctor and my jacket. But I could not bring myself to tell Collie about that at the moment.

"Go back to this morning now," he urged, "and tell me just exactly what you did and what you and Billy Ray said to each other."

So I tried to remember every little detail from the time we drove down the lane in my car and exchanged it for his car on through the morning till the time Billy Ray left me back in my car at the lane. When I had finished, Collie was ready with questions, mainly about the times when Billy Ray and I were away from each other during the morning. He was interested in how long it had taken him to hide my car and reappear in his own at the parsonage and in which directions he had gone when we separated at various times. He was particularly concerned with the fact that he did not stay with me while I was reading in the library.

"I would be willing to bet most any amount that the good reverend went back to that drugstore and retrieved those two rolls of film," he said.

"Why?"

"Because there is a photographer in town who will develop film in just a couple of hours. I have an idea that Brother Johnson will pick up those pictures this afternoon," he said, "and weed out any that he doesn't want you to see."

"There won't be anything in that film that David would mind anybody else seeing," I said confidently, remembering that he had told the motel woman to hand it to me even if I were not alone.

My tone of voice was so confident that Collie snapped to attention at once. "How do you know?" he asked. I, of course, had not mentioned the other envelope or Billy Ray searching my purse or the doctor's concern with my jacket. "What happened that you haven't told me?" he insisted gravely.

Until I had a chance to play that tape I could not tell anyone about it, not even him, but I saw that I had to tell him something. "I think Billy Ray believes David left something other than the film somewhere," I said, "and there's something else." I hesitated.

"Well, go on," he insisted.

"I know you'll find it hard to believe," I said.

He was growing impatient. "Do try telling me and let's see."

"I think Doc Perkins might be mixed up in whatever it is."

He laughed. "You're seeing villains behind every bush. I've known Doc Perkins all my life. Every bit of my life. Why in the world would you think he is involved?"

"I told you you wouldn't believe me." I fear that I pouted a bit as I said that.

"Come on, Anne," he said, smiling through clenched teeth, "why do you think he is mixed up in this?"

So I told him about going into the sunroom and having to go to the bathroom, still leaving out about the tape, and how the doctor had tried to search my jacket before he left. Collie's face grew serious. He stood up and walked over to the stream. Bottom had wandered back to lie down near us but jumped up to follow him, thinking a new game was about to start.

"I'm sorry, Collie," I said, going over to stand beside him. "Maybe I was imagining things."

He shook his head and kicked at a clump of green moss near the stream. "No, " he said, "that could explain lots of things, although I hate to believe it's true."

I put my hand on his arm and he reached over and moved it down to clasp with his own. I decided that I should also tell him about the ghosts in Marley's rooms so I went through the whole tale including my theory that I had heard two different sounds.

He confirmed my theory by saying, "If you did hear the sounds that night, it's the first time anyone has reported hearing them in your room."

I looked up at him, surprised. He continued, "The only rooms in the house where there is any record of the singing occurring are the rooms you saw where Marley insisted on having her apartment and a trunk room on the third floor directly over

those.   Marley thought she could get rid of the
ghosts by lowering the ceiling and building new
walls in her rooms, but she couldn't and that's when
she installed the music system which drowns out the
sounds."

I had to know his reaction to that suite. "Did
you live in those rooms?"

"No," he answered simply. "She had them decorated just before I moved out to the carriage
house," he paused. "I had promised to let her have
two rooms to do with as she pleased if she would
move to Goldengrove with me. I thought the old
house might help straighten out our marriage, but I
guess it was hopeless. Especially after she met Billy
Ray Johnson." His voice was bitter.

I didn't think either of us felt like discussing
those rooms any further so I changed the subject
back to my problem. "Do you think I might find out
anything at the post office? And do you have any
idea as to where David's car might be?"

"I don't know to both questions," he said shaking his head. "I have a friend at the post office who
checked the general delivery mail for me to see if
perhaps David mailed himself a letter or perhaps
one to his family or to anyone for that matter, but
with no luck. And I have gone to every place in
town that rents parking space; also, I have driven up
and down every street in town to see if his car might

be abandoned somewhere. Again with no luck. You see, David told me on Friday that he had come up with something on Wednesday night that he thought I would like to know and asked if he could come out Sunday night to talk with me about it after he sorted through his notes and checked out something that was bothering him."

He had turned to face me and was now holding my hand in both of his. "When he didn't appear on Sunday night, I called the motel and found that he had left. I called the other motels out on the highway and even called Billy Ray to ask if he knew anything about him. The way he talked that night convinced me that he knew something he wasn't telling me, and I still think he does." He turned from me and went back to the table. "Nothing that preacher could do would surprise me. Nothing. But I just can't face Doc Perkins being involved."

"Why don't you like Billy Ray?" I asked. Perhaps I shouldn't ask, I was telling myself, but I wanted to hear what he would say, and was more than shocked by his terse answer.

"I'll tell it briefly," he said. "Billy Ray's mother married my father a year before he died when he was already a sick old man, and she and Billy Ray connived to get his will changed—unsuccessfully, I'm glad to say. And then when Marley and I moved to Goldengrove he started in after her.

Successfully."

"I'm sorry," I said simply. "Where is his mother now?"

"She had the good grace to take the nice sum of money Papa left her and disappear from my life."

I was walking back over to join him at the table when we heard Miss Lucy screaming Collie's name from the house.

"My God, what now!" he exclaimed and set off running toward the shouts.

Bottom and I followed with me running as fast as I dared to keep from falling on my broken arm and with Bottom loping along beside me. We caught up as he was standing at the back door trying to calm down Miss Lucy enough to tell him what was the matter.

Caroline rushed up at the same time, saying that she had heard all the yelling over at the carriage house.

Miss Lucy was pointing toward the upstairs and saying Miss Allie's name over and over, so Collie dashed on into the house with Bottom at his heels. Caroline and I led Miss Lucy into the kitchen for a glass of water.

I was debating with myself whether or not to follow Collie up the stairs when we heard him calling down to us. He told Caroline to call Doc Perkins to come back at once and he told me to come up to help him. That settled my debate about following him, so I hurried up the stairs.

He was already rushing down the hallway so I ran to catch up with him, which I did just as he was turning onto the passageway and heading for the open door to my room. He stopped for a moment and told me to brace myself. I tried to, but I was not prepared for the sight in my room: Miss Allie was lying face down on the floor with a gash in the back of her white head from which a stream of blood was dripping onto the golden carpet.

"Get a towel," Collie ordered. I rushed into the bathroom and grabbed a clean towel which he used to try to stop the bleeding. He also pulled a blanket from my bed and wrapped it around the old woman, being careful not to move her. She was breathing, but she was lying awfully still.

Caroline came in and told us that Dr. Perkins' nurse said he was still in the neighborhood and she would contact him at once. Caroline knelt beside Miss Allie, took one of the outstretched hands and sat gently patting the limp vein-corded old white hand with her own soft brown ones. Miss Lucy, calm and in control again, followed soon and sat in the rocker. For a moment we were like figures in a wax museum tableau and then Collie asked Miss Lucy to tell us what happened.

It seemed that Miss Allie had become disgusted

with the plot of her soap and had decided to read, but could not find the magazine she wanted downstairs. Miss Lucy offered to go upstairs to hunt down the magazine for her, but she insisted on going herself, saying that the exercise would do her good. When she did not return in fifteen minutes or so, Miss Lucy called up the stairs and getting no answer went up and found her lying this way in my room. Miss Lucy had heard no noise.

Bottom was sniffing around the room and started pawing at something near the fireplace. I went over and found that my purse was lying on the floor where it had obviously been tossed. I remembered leaving it on the bed when I had come in earlier.

"See if anything is missing but leave it there," said Collie. I checked my wallet and found that all of the money I had had in the main compartment, about ninety dollars, was gone. Everything else was there including some money I had stuck among my credit cards. I walked around the room, quietly looking and found that here a drawer was not quite closed and there a book had been shoved to one side. The pillows on my bed were not quite in place and the armoire door was slightly open. Someone had searched my room very carefully and very thoroughly. I caught Collie's eye and he shook his head so I didn't mention this to the others.

Miss Lucy went into her room to check her

purse and came back saying that about twenty dollars was missing and then she went out and around the passageway to Miss Allie's room and reported back that Miss Allie's purse was lying in the middle of the floor and that her change purse was lying empty beside it.

The back doorbell chimed about then and we heard Dr. Perkins calling from downstairs. Miss Lucy hastened to the back stairway and told him to come up, and Collie asked me to sit on the floor and hold the towel on Miss Allie's head while he called the sheriff. As Caroline and I huddled on the floor beside Miss Allie, again everything seemed to float into slow motion. How had I managed to get into such a situation as this? And would this rosy little woman die because my brother and I had come into her world? I could not believe that someone had actually hit Miss Allie's white head. Certainly whoever did it didn't do it for the few dollars he found in our purses. Could that tape lying among the tissues a few feet from us be so important that a little old lady's head should be bashed in? I shuddered and wondered why the doctor didn't hurry.

No more than a few moments could have passed since we heard his voice downstairs, but it was an eternity to me, especially after Collie left the room. As long as he was there, I kept my panic in check, but my self-control left the room when he did. I looked all around the room again and each little thing I saw out of place seemed to grow in size and importance until it looked to me as though the whole place was a shambles. But no one else had noticed a thing wrong, and Collie seemed not to want to worry the others with it. Bottom came over and stood beside me, laying his soft chin on my shoulder and whining a little in my ear.

Then Miss Lucy was leading the doctor into the room, telling him what had happened as they walked. And Collie was hurrying back in saying the sheriff was on his way. My face must have been as pale as my thoughts because he came over to help me to my feet as the doctor knelt beside poor Miss Allie. I murmured something about being sick and went into the bathroom, locking both doors. I again ran the water in the lavatory and felt down into the tissue box.

The tape was still there.

But now I was panicky about what to do with that tissue box. If I left it there, would whoever came looking for the tape come back and go over the bathroom? I decided that now was no time to try to move it. I was so shaky that I would probably just drop the tape in full view if I even tried to carry it across the room, so I left it there on the commode and gave a sigh of relief. I must have stayed longer than I had intended because Miss Lucy called out to ask if I was all right. I answered that I would hurry and splashed some cold water on my face and hastily dried it off. Then I went back into my room.

The doctor had just finished giving Miss Allie a shot of some sort and was shaking his head solemnly. I went over to stand beside Collie. In the distance we heard a siren and then another and the wails of both soon whined to a stop at Goldengrove's back door.

"I asked Maude to send the ambulance on over since it sounded like we'd need it," said Dr. Perkins, snapping shut his black bag and getting to his feet. "Lucy, get your coat and ride in the ambulance with Allie so Collie can drive his car. I'll go on ahead and meet you all at the hospital."

As the doctor went out my door, the sheriff came in followed by two ambulance people with their stretcher.

The sheriff was a large red-faced man with a soft voice. He told the two attendants to get Miss Allie to the hospital at once so they picked up the still little lady and hurried out with Miss Lucy at their heels. Caroline came back in with some sort of cleaner and started removing the blood from the carpet. My head was aching so I sat down by the fireplace and called Bottom over to sit beside me out of the way.

"How did you get out here so fast?" asked

Collie of the sheriff.

"I was on my way out to the preacher's house across the road when your call came in," he answered. "Seems somebody robbed him just before they got you all so he had already called me. He's missing some money and a watch, so I came on here since nobody was hurt over at his house." He got out a notebook and asked Collie for details on what happened.

I interrupted to ask if Billy Ray Johnson had seen the thief and the sheriff assured me that he had seen a man run from his yard over in our direction and then a few minutes later had seen someone in an old pickup drive by, but he hadn't been able to catch him or to see him well enough to file a description.

When I heard this, I thought maybe I just imagined that someone searched my room. Maybe it was only a matter of a passing thief and I had heard Collie say that the front door was never locked in the daytime so that would explain how the thief had entered. I wanted desperately to believe that poor Miss Allie had not been hurt as a result of my being at Goldengrove, but something inside told me that Billy Ray Johnson had been in this room and had reported a robbery at his house only to convince the sheriff that a passing thief did in fact go through both houses. Who would ever believe me if I said the minister had lied? And, of course, there was always the possibility that he had not lied and that he indeed was not involved in anything other than caring for his flock. My head ached more and more and the whole nightmare whirled around me until my mind seemed to belong to somebody else.

The sheriff was leaving and Collie was asking if I wanted to go with him back to town to the hospital, but he did not seem surprised that I didn't want to go. I asked him to leave me to rest and pull myself together. He was reluctant about leaving me but Caroline assured him she would stay with me. For a moment, as he was standing there worrying about leaving me, I felt that I was making a mistake not telling him about the tape, but then he was gone and I hadn't told him.

It was after four o'clock by now and the sun was already beginning to set, making the elm grove more golden than ever as I stood at my window and watched the black Cadillac move off.

I have often wondered since then just what might have happened if I had gone to the Blue Valley Hospital with Collie that afternoon. Perhaps the events which followed his departure from Goldengrove would have happened later and been worse. But as I stood at that window and watched him leave, I couldn't help feeling that in spite of Caroline I was all alone in this haunted house with no protection from whatever evil was at work in it. And somehow I knew the key to the whole situation lay in the tape David had left for me, but until I had heard it, I could not entrust it to anyone else. What if David's life depended on that little spool?

I told myself that I was being overly dramatic and tried to shake the cobwebs from my brain and think about what I should do while waiting to hear from Collie. Caroline had gone downstairs after cleaning the carpet saying that she would make us a pot of coffee. Somehow I had to find a tape recorder and hear that tape.

Then all of a sudden I remembered that I had seen a tape player right there in the house: On a black-lacquered library table in Marley's sitting room stood a typewriter and a tape recorder. It was a small one and certainly portable even for someone with a broken arm. So I smiled at the thought of how simple it would be to slip into that room and bring the machine back to the bathroom, play the tape then return the machine.

But first I would rush downstairs and drink the coffee; then I would insist that Caroline go on home, never thinking that I would really be alone, only feeling excitement that at last I could discover some clue to David's whereabouts.

Caroline made my plan easier by asking if I would be afraid to stay alone while she ran over to the carriage house and turned off some appliances she had left on when she rushed out. She assured me that she had locked all of the outside doors in the house and that the sheriff had helped her check all the rooms to make sure no one was hiding there. She said she would also go tell her husband where she was and what had happened and then bring him back to the house with her and they would prepare some supper. I convinced her that not only would I not be afraid, but I would welcome an opportunity to take a little nap since the day had really been tiring for me. And anyway, I had Bottom to keep me company.

So I locked the back door behind Caroline and called Bottom to go upstairs with me, but first I turned on most of the lights downstairs because it was almost dark outside—and darker than that in the heavily-draped mansion. Bottom whined a bit as if he didn't much want to go upstairs, but I called him a sissy and hurried on up with him at my heels.

Of course, my plan was too simple. The door to Marley's sitting room was locked.

I was furious and puzzled. The door had been unlocked the night before, probably left that way by Caroline the last time she cleaned. Who had locked it? I told myself that the door was probably kept locked all the time and Caroline had just forgotten to relock it. Maybe the catch had failed to make connection when she shut the door but did catch when I closed it so firmly on leaving the rooms.

And then I remembered that the roof of the carport was right under the windows on the back of the house so I sped down to the end of the hallway and, sure enough, the window would open and on leaning out, I saw that I could easily walk over to the window in Marley's bedroom. But I had to hurry.

Climbing through windows would not be easy for me to do with a broken arm, I realized, and indeed, I did find it a difficult task to heave myself up onto the ledge and swing out onto the roof. I closed the window behind me and felt lucky that the Goldengrove folks didn't believe in locking windows and doors—except the doors to that depressing suite—even though Caroline and the sheriff were supposed to have locked up the place. I found that the bedroom window was unlocked and not difficult to raise. I reached in first and found the cord to draw open the curtains in order to let in enough light to guide me to a light switch and then again went through the process of hauling myself up and over the ledge, wishing that the French doors on the front of the house were around here also.

I had left Bottom whining in the hall, standing under the window I had climbed out, very unhappy that I insisted he not follow me. I was so anxious to get my hands on a tape machine it didn't occur to me to remember how terrified I had been in Marley's rooms with Bottom along, but now as I stepped into that bizarre bedroom made even more bizarre by the twilight haze, I wished for a moment I had let him climb through the windows with me.

But I had no time for wishes. Here I was within a few feet of the machine that might lead me to David so I rushed across the bedroom and turned on the overhead light, then went back to close the window and the awful orange drapes. When I turned to go to the sitting room, I saw that a closet door stood open where I hadn't even realized there was a closet. And beside that door was another one open into what was obviously a bathroom. I was surprised but thought that maybe the night before I had just been too shocked to notice the doors and sped on into the sitting room, turning out the bedroom light as soon as I had pressed the switch just inside the other room.

The tape recorder was sitting just where I remembered it and I snatched it up and held it under my broken arm so I could open the door, turn out the light and leave, all the while almost talking out loud, telling myself just what to do at each step of the way. I made sure that the door did not lock behind me because I knew that I must replace the machine at once after I had heard the tape.

Bottom bounded down the hall from the window where he had been keeping watch and greeted me happily. Together we returned to my room where I locked the door and then also locked the French doors onto the balcony before going into the bathroom.

I found a plug for the machine and put it on a little stool and carefully removed the reel from its hiding place. With some difficulty in my one-handed fashion I placed the tape on the sprocket and threaded it onto the empty spool. Then I turned on the water—I don't know why I kept thinking the walls in Goldengrove might have ears—and with the volume very low, I leaned down close to the machine and pushed the Play button.

The tape slithered smoothly along its track as I held my breath waiting for a sound. And then David's voice spoke:

"Spliced segments to contrast contrived ghost singing and real ghost singing. Number 1 always contrived. Number 2 always real."

David had also heard two sets of ghost singing.

There were several segments of each type of singing, and before each segment David's voice stated either "Number 1" or "Number 2." I recognized the sounds from the first segments as those I had heard in my room and the second group were like those I had heard in Marley's suite—muted and with an indistinct tune whereas the first group had an almost recognizable tune. This comparison went on for a few minutes and then David announced that the following was a recording of the ghosts singing on the date of the past Friday night, the night before our last strange telephone conversation.

A space of silence followed and then the eerie rising and falling of sound picked up and continued, now faint and then louder as if the tape machine were being moved from place to place during the singing. I was sure that was what was going on because at one point there were the sounds of something falling over and a muffled exclamation.

The reel of tape had almost run out and I was beginning to wonder why all the secrecy about this bit of plastic when the back of my neck started tingling. Definite words were coming through the singing. Someone was talking in the background. I leaned still closer to listen after rewinding the tape a few feet, then playing it again.

I still couldn't understand those first few words; they sounded far in the distance and also on top of them and the singing there was a rushing sound as though David may have hidden behind something when he heard the voices. They were definitely human voices and there seemed to be two of them, two men. Finally I caught what they were saying.

"—don't like it. How can you be sure he won't come in?"

"He told me the old lady had given him permission to spend the night in the trunk room. Bring that box on in and put it with the others."

"I still think we should have left them in the tunnel."

"That's not practical right now. Andrews almost caught me the other night with a shipment. He's suspected for some time that something's going on. He'll never look at anything in this room and with the stuff here, we can always point the authorities to him in case he tries to blow the whistle on me."

"It's beginning to stack up."

"I know, but I've been afraid to get rid of it on my trips since that Whitehead fellow has been nosing around. I don't think he's anything more than a graduate student, but we can't take any chances. Tomorrow he's moving in with me. One false move on his part and I arrange an accident for David and send the sheriff to check on Andrews."

Billy Ray Johnson was talking with Doc Perkins. Why hadn't I trusted Collie enough to let him hear this tape?

"I'm getting too old to be involved in things like

this."

"Well, you've just about paid off that old debt with the money you've gotten, haven't you?"

"Yes, but here I am helping you deal in heroin which hurts the humanity I swore to heal."

"Hell, Doc, they'd get it from somebody else if we didn't do it. And at least you're not having to hide behind a pulpit like I am. Another few thousand in the bank and I think I'll leave the country."

The next sentence was lost as if a door had closed between David and the two men.

The tape ran off its reel and flapped noisily as the take-up spool spun around and around for a few seconds until I realized that I must stop the machine and rewind the tape. My hands were so clammy and cold that I could hardly persuade my clumsy left one to perform, but finally I had the thing rewound and the reel back in its box and hidden again among the tissues.

And now I had to go back into that suite and replace the tape machine. I decided that I must do that task and then think about what I had heard; otherwise, I might never get up the courage to return to those rooms. So I picked up the tape recorder and sped back to leave it where I had found it. At any moment I fully expected to be grabbed and hauled off, but I made the trip there and back safely and once back in my room paced back and forth thinking and worrying about what I had heard.

Somehow Billy Ray must have found out that David had been in Marley's rooms. And David must have told him about the tape in order to avoid the "accident," thinking that he would be safe as long as Billy Ray was looking for it. But why had he not told Collie the whole story? What threat was hanging over his head? And where was my brother now if he was still alive?

A tunnel. Doc Perkins had mentioned a tunnel. That must have been how the two men had entered the room where David heard them talking. And it had to be in Marley's rooms because Collie had told me that the only two places anyone had heard the ghosts were there and in the trunk room where Billy Ray had thought David to be. Obviously the false singing was something Billy Ray had rigged to throw David off in his work and used later to try to frighten me away or to do whatever his twisted mind had invented. I knew I had to do something fast.

What I had to do was find a flashlight and hunt for the passageway out of those rooms and find that tunnel. I couldn't help hoping that was where I would find David.

I hurriedly slipped out of my skirt and into a pair of slacks. Then I shut Bottom up in my room and rushed downstairs to see if I could find a flashlight. I was rummaging around in a kitchen drawer when the telephone rang.

A thought occurred to me as I went to answer the phone: Suppose it had been Billy Ray who struck Miss Allie and she had seen him. If the blow didn't kill her, the doctor could do so easily with an injection. The extension I picked up was in the sun-room and I saw someone coming up to the back door as I said hello.

Collie started out by telling me that Miss Allie was alive but still unconscious. I interrupted him rudely. Billy Ray Johnson was knocking on the back door, a fragile glass door.

"Get another doctor," I whispered. And added "The tissue box in my bathroom."

Then I hung up the phone and was about to run upstairs and barricade myself in my room when I saw that Caroline and her husband had also come up to the back door and were waiting with the minister to be let in. I rushed over to open the door and heard to my horror that the preacher was telling them to leave.

"I was just saying that I have cooked you a nice dinner to make up for the one we didn't eat at noon," he told me with a large smile. "Doc Perkins called to tell me about poor Miss Allie and asked me to check on you."

I started to plead a headache but Caroline was insisting that what I needed was a good hot meal.

"I'll run up and get my purse," I said.

But Billy Ray took my arm and held it firmly. "Caroline, would you please bring her purse down so she won't have to climb all those stairs again?"

Of course she would and there went my chance to hide. And then I saw that Caroline's husband had already gone and I didn't dare say anything to endanger her, so all I could do was smile and look pale hoping that I could manage to hide my fear of Billy Ray and for David.

I tried once more. "Maybe I should get my coat," I said.

He walked over to the stairway with me and called up to Caroline to bring the coat. So I decided to play innocent.

"That was Collie on the phone," I said. "Miss Allie is still unconscious but at least she's alive."

His grip on my arm relaxed. "The doctor told me that she was hit on the head. Did it look like a bad thing?"

I shuddered, for more than one reason. "Terrible," I answered, "but we hope we got to her in time. I don't think she lost an awful lot of blood."

"That's good," he said. "I'll run in to the hospital tomorrow to visit her."

Caroline came back downstairs on the tail end of that statement and I repeated Collie's report on Miss Allie to her. She shook her head sadly and handed me my purse and put the coat around my shoulders.

"Come on, Caroline," said Billy Ray, "and let us give you a ride down the lane."

"What if the professor calls in again and finds us gone?" she asked. "Maybe I should stay here."

"I'll have Anne back here before he calls again or comes in. We'll just eat supper and then I'll bring her back and send her up to bed," he said smiling sweetly down on me. "I know she's worn out by all this." And he started gently shepherding us out the door.

"Oh," I said casually, "I don't have a key."

"There's one under the doormat," said Caroline and leaned down to make sure the key was in place.

"Fine," said our genial escort, "we're all set." And he very solicitously put us into his car and away we went.

At the end of the lane Caroline got out and told me to call her if I needed her to come back to stay with me. "My number is on the pad by the sunroom phone," she said.

As if that will do me a lot of good, I thought. But aloud I thanked her and swallowed hard as she shut the door and waited for us to move on off so she could cross the road to her house, whose lights I could see in the near distance.

There was a sudden muggy warmth in the air

and the dark was dense among the trees. The day had been filled with so many things that I felt it should be midnight instead of only six. I sighed.

"What's the matter?" asked Billy Ray, still keeping up the game.

"It feels like rain again," I said. "Does it always rain so much up here?"

He laughed "Not always, but we get our share. And more sometimes. But you should be used to rain in New Orleans."

I braced myself for the turn into his driveway. "Somehow the rain doesn't seem so wet when it falls on concrete as it does falling on grass," I said.

I guess he was confident that I would not try to run away because instead of insisting that I get out on his side as he had made me enter the car, he got out and went around to my side, moving rather slowly as if his leg were bothering him. I started sliding across the seat toward his door as soon as he closed it and by the time he reached my door, I had my left hand on the handle of his door and was out of the car and running across his front yard before he realized what was going on.

I could hear him limping along behind me on the driveway and he called out to me, "Anne, you'd better come back and tell me where it is or you'll never see David again."

I almost stopped and went back, but somehow I

felt that if I did, I would really never see David again because once Billy Ray got that tape he would not be able to turn either one of us loose. So I sped on, running faster than I knew I could across the road and then slowing down to find the low brick wall. I crawled over it and by now my eyes were almost accustomed to the blackness around me and I was able to distinguish the tree trunks in the elm grove. Behind me I heard Billy Ray start his car and gun the motor.

As I picked my way among the trees, I was hoping Billy Ray would think I had headed for Caroline's house. I stopped a moment and wondered if I had any chance of beating him up the hill to the back door, and if I did, was I playing into his hands by going there. But where else was there for me to go?

He had come out of his driveway and was driving slowly along the road shining a flashlight first on one side of the road and then the other. He couldn't risk letting me reach Caroline's house on that side or Goldengrove on this one. The beam was too short to pick me up so far away, but I was afraid he would hear me running in the thick leaves if I moved too rapidly so I started up again, moving as slowly as I could and as quietly as I could and still make some progress.

He stopped his car at the gate and got out to listen. I stopped as soon as the engine died and tried to slow my heavy panting which sounded awfully loud to me. I had made good time in my sprint and was about halfway up the hill and over toward the church side of the grove, but I was still afraid to make any noise, so I stood behind a tree, peeking out from time to time to keep up with what he was doing.

He started walking toward the back of the car, shining his flashlight across the road toward Caroline's house.

I raised a foot and started to take a step forward but the rustling of the leaves sounded like gunfire, so I brought that foot back down on top of my other one and held my breath to see if Billy Ray had heard me. He obviously had not because he was walking on around the car slowly, combing the area with his light.

In the distance a dog barked and another one answered. The usual night sounds went on but not loudly enough to cover any sounds I might make.

Billy Ray got back into his car and started the engine, and the minute it caught I rushed forward. He stopped in front of the carriage house and did his light-shining bit but this time he did not kill the engine, so I kept going from tree to tree, but more slowly while he was stopped.

And then I was nearly to the cleared lawn in

front of Goldengrove where light was shining from most of the windows downstairs. Luckily for me though, I had forgotten to turn on the outside lights so I still had some darkness going for me as I sprinted for the shadows on the side of the house.

I heard the car come on around and stop in the carport before I could reach the back door. I flattened myself against the house and heard him fumble for the key under the doormat and open the door. I was close enough to hear him rush in to the telephone. Through the door he had not closed I could hear him talking, obviously to Caroline.

"I've brought her on back," he said, "because she was too tired to eat. Said she'd just go to bed and to ask you to tell them not to disturb her."

I didn't wait to hear more. I raced back around the house and racked my brain for a place to hide. I left the shadow of the house and plunged into the darkness over toward the church and came abruptly to the brick wall again, so I climbed over it and crouched down to rest a minute and try to think of places Billy Ray might look for me. I heard the back door slam and saw him limp out to the garage. And then he came out of the garage and started around the house toward me. My heart was pounding so hard I was afraid he must be able to hear it.

But all of a sudden he stopped in his tracks and turned oft the flashlight and then I heard it.

The whole hill was alive with the sound that had started out as a thin wail and was now a congregation of tones spiraling from high to low and intermingling until it seemed as if the very skies were alive. A wind blew up and the elms joined in, rattling their leaves in rhythm with the ghost chorus. As I covered my mouth with my hand to keep from crying out, I heard Billy Ray Johnson utter a short extra-loud exclamation. He turned the flashlight back on and used it to guide himself back around to his car which he brought to life and drove back down the lane and turned in the direction of the Crossroads.

The ghost singing stopped abruptly and the wind died down in the elms. I listened for the sound of Billy Ray's car speeding off down the graveled road because I was afraid he might stop and come back. Sure enough, the car sounds died out before he had time to go very far, and I knew that he was on his way back.

I was on my feet about to climb back over the wall to run for the house when I realized that this was just exactly what he was giving me a chance to do. He wanted me in the house where he could corner me. There was no telling where the secret passages went, but he would know and be able to get to me where I least expected him. What could I do now?

I looked back toward Goldengrove, elegant in the night with its windows aglow and then I caught my breath. The light in my room suddenly went out and came back on dimmer, as if someone had turned out the overhead and switched on a lamp.

And over on the lane I could hear Billy Ray Johnson limping toward the house as fast as his leg and the cane would let him.

I sat down on the ground and leaned against the rough bricks of the wall, waiting for Billy Ray to reach the house before moving again. It was nice to have the ghosts on my side if that was what had turned the lights off and on in my room. For some reason it didn't seem far-fetched to me at that moment that there were really ghosts at Goldengrove, and I even more or less wished they would tell me what to do about a place to hide.

Ghosts indeed. I was not convinced like David was that there were such things, but after what I had heard and seen at Goldengrove, I knew that I would never again be so loudly skeptical of them. At the moment, however, I needed to think of some way to find that tunnel.

Far away thunder growled and the reflection from a distant lightning flash illuminated the hillside, outlining the dark little church and its tiny cemetery. As the darkness closed in again, I remembered seeing the bobbing light in the churchyard, and here where I could judge distances better, I realized that the light had gone toward the tombstones and that when it had disappeared out in the yard, it must have been among them. The entrance to the tunnel must be in that ancient graveyard. But how could I look for it without a flashlight? Would it be easier to slip back into the house and try to find the entrance to it from Marley's rooms? For obviously, according to the tape, one of the secret passages in the house had to give entry to that tunnel.

But I couldn't run the risk of bumping into Billy Ray Johnson inside the house.

I would have to forget about a light and just take my chances in the dark.

There was a fairly clear space of perhaps seventy-five feet between my place by the wall and the little patch of tombstones, so, certain that Billy Ray had had time to be inside the house, I got to my feet and started out. The air began to smell like rain, and a drop or two spattered on me as I ran, but fortunately the storm was going to circle round us that night and a wind was blowing the thick clouds away. Once when I looked up, I even saw an opening large enough for a few stars to shine through.

Finally I reached the iron fence and stopped for breath. The insect chorus commented on my being there and suddenly coming from out of nowhere, a cat rubbed against my legs just about sending me up among those stars. It was a very friendly animal and meowed loudly at me, but I finally convinced it with an unfriendly, but necessary, kick to go on and leave me alone. In the next bit of light I saw it racing across the yard toward the church.

I also saw that there were four large brick pillars holding the fence up, one pillar at each corner. I felt my way to the one on my left and found that a gate was attached to it. The gate was locked with a huge padlock. And the fence was something like four feet high and made of iron pickets. The padlock was old and rusty, so I decided that wherever the tunnel entrance was, it wasn't on the other side of that gate. And the bobbing light had been in view until it disappeared. Consequently, one of the two pillars on the house side of the cemetery must be what I was seeking. Something inside me breathed a sigh of relief that I didn't have to go inside the graveyard. Whether or not I believed in ghosts, I did not relish the idea of stomping around on somebody's grave in the black of night.

The pillars were something like two feet square and made of the same rough old brick as the wall around Goldengrove.

I stood by the one at the gate and felt around over as much of its surface as I could reach with my one hand and found nothing, so I moved on down to the one at the back corner and started the same process. I had broken just about every fingernail on that poor overworked left hand and found nothing so I gave a disgusted sigh and leaned on the pillar. I was surprised when I felt it move, so I leaned against it harder and it swung smoothly to my right and there at my feet was a dimly lighted hole with a ladder inside. I mentally praised Billy Ray for having the thing wired for light and leaned down to look before climbing in. All I could see was that the ladder went down about eight feet into some sort of room.

I pitched my purse and coat in and scampered down the ladder but very nearly lost my nerve when I hit the bottom rung and the pillar moved shut above me. I stood back up on that rung and the pillar opened, so I breathed more easily when it closed a second time.

I found myself in a room about ten feet square lined with shelves on three sides. On the fourth side, in addition to about four feet of shelves, there was a tunnel leading off the room.

As I became accustomed to the dim light, I saw that there was a cot over on the other side of the ladder with a bundle of blankets on it. A small electric heater had taken the chill off the room, but it was still very cold down there. As I stooped to pick up my coat and purse, I saw the blankets move a bit and knew that I had found my brother.

I dashed over and pulled back the cover from his head, If I hadn't seen the blankets move, I would have thought him dead from the paleness of his face and the slackness of his features.

I shook him and called his name softly, but he was obviously drugged. There was a half-empty plate of food on the straw-covered floor near his head. Looking around the room, I saw a bottle of pills on one of the shelves which were, in fact, empty except for that bottle. There were a few clean square marks in the dust where something had been sitting on the shelves until recently. I turned back to David and pulled all the cover off him. He was wearing his favorite red pullover and a pair of jeans. His right wrist was handcuffed to the iron cot and his ankles were tied together firmly. On the other side of the cot stood a smelly covered pot that had been put there obviously for his use and for his ingenuity to figure out just how to get to it.

I agitated his free hand and patted his face and finally his eyes opened. I tried to pull him to a sitting position but was not strong enough to do it one-handed.

"David," I begged, "please wake up." I could tell that although his eyes were open, he couldn't focus them. "It's Anne. Wake up, David."

He shook his head feebly and closed his eyes tightly, then opened them again, obviously trying to shake the drug's effects. "Wake up, David," I said again and slapped his cheeks. Tears began to roll down my face from sheer relief and frustration and fatigue. "Please, David," I sobbed, "wake up."

Finally he screwed up his face, opened one eye and recognized me. And then he fell back into that coma-like sleep. I let him turn on his side and covered him up. At least he was alive. Now all I had to do was figure out how to get him loose and out of that hole.

I walked over and looked into the tunnel which was about five feet high and a little over four feet wide and I was about to go into it to see if it was lighted around the bend I could see a few feet in, when I heard a shuffling noise in the distance.

It must be Billy Ray Johnson coming through. I hurriedly grabbed my purse and coat and frantically looked for a place to hide. The only thing in the room was the cot so I would have to get under it. I rolled under the low bed, wincing as I hit my broken arm, and pulled at David's blankets until there was some cloth hanging down to hide me. He muttered in his sleep and I was petrified for fear he would really wake up at this point. I closed my eyes tightly and held my breath as I heard Billy Ray come in. I realized that closing my eyes would not keep him from seeing me so I opened them and saw his feet go over to one of the shelves, then turn and return to the tunnel. As I heard his steps retreat, I peered out and saw two small square boxes sitting on a shelf.

He was moving the heroin out of the house. Or maybe he was just moving part of it. And was planning to use what was left in the house to frame Collie.

I had to leave that hole in the ground and contact Collie. And now was my chance while the preacher was in the tunnel. I slid out from under the cot and David stirred in his sleep. I shook him again and whispered in his ear that I would be back, and holding my coat and purse under my cast, I stepped on the lower rung of the ladder.

I don't remember climbing up the ladder, but I know that I was up and out of that place fast.

It was darker than ever outside so I had to fumble around to push the pillar back into place. Just as it closed over the opening something rushed at me from behind and I fell over. Strong arms grabbed me as I fell and a very wet tongue in a fuzzy face started licking my cheek.

Collie and Bottom had found me.

Chapter Six

"Down, dog," said the professor. "It's my turn to kiss her." And he did before setting me on my feet. And again tears were all over my face. It was very frustrating because I had always prided myself on being strong and untearful in critical situations. But here I was out of that tunnel room back with Collie and Bottom and I knew that David was alive, but I didn't know how we were going to manage to rescue him. So I dug some tissues out of a pocket and blew my nose and pulled Collie away from the post, shushing Bottom who was leaping around us in noisy glee.

The clouds had gone and the night was clear and much colder than it had been earlier. When we reached the wall, I stopped and asked how they had found me.

"Bottom found you," Collie said, rubbing the

happy head. "Caroline called when she saw my car lights and said that you were asleep which I thought strange after your cryptic message. And then I heard Bottom barking in your room."

"Did you find the tape?"

"Yes," he said, "as much as I hated to delay looking for you, I thought I had better find out what this was all about first. Bottom was furious with me for not rushing to your rescue at once. But I ran into the room I've been using and played the tape and then called the sheriff. As soon as I let Bottom out of your room, he led me around the yard and into the grove, then flew over here and started digging around that post where you appeared."

I shivered and he pulled me closer to him. "That's where the tunnel comes out," I whispered, "and that's where David is." I was frantic to get David out of that room. "We must hurry." But he held me firmly there.

"So that was his do-it-yourself project," he muttered half to himself. "Restoring the passages—and I guess he found the tunnel in the process."

"His project?" I asked.

"The good Reverend. He lived at Goldengrove while his mother was here, and my dad let him do as he pleased. Papa was too sick to care what went on the last few months and Billy Ray came near to doing me out of Goldengrove itself," he said bitterly. "But for now tell me what happened. What we need to do is wait for the sheriff and help him save David and find Billy Ray with the heroin."

So I told him how I had found the opening to the underground room and gave him a quick blow-by-blow of what had gone on while I was there with David. "I'm sure Billy Ray has some sort of plan to escape and leave you looking guilty," I said, "and I'm so afraid he'll kill David before he leaves."

I was growing impatient. How could we stand out here under these stars discussing the situation when David's life was in danger? But underneath I knew Collie was right and that we would spoil everything by rushing in and trying to overpower Billy Ray Johnson.

We stood there holding onto each other and Bottom was glad to stay beside us. And finally I asked about Miss Allie.

"She's all right, thanks to you," Collie said bitterly.

"Doc Perkins?"

"He was about to give her some sort of lethal injection when I rushed back to her room after talking with you." Collie had trouble telling me this tale and my heart went out to him. "I think he was already in a state of shock over what he was about to do, and when he saw me, he collapsed with a heart attack. That's why I was delayed getting back."

"Will he be all right?" I asked.

Collie sighed. "No, they don't think he'll last the night, but he told me before I left that Billy Ray was blackmailing him about something in his past and also that Miss Allie saw Billy Ray just before he hit her."

"Will you tell Miss Allie?" I whispered.

"Not about Doc if I can help it," he answered tensely. "But after we catch Billy Ray, I'm sure he'll whine it all out to everybody."

We waited. Only a very few minutes had passed, I'm sure, when we heard a car turn into the lane and glide to a stop near the carriage house. About that time I grabbed Bottom and pulled him and Collie down into the shadow of the wall because I had heard a faint sound from the cemetery. The pillar swung back and Billy Ray quickly emerged and closed the opening behind him. We could tell he was empty-handed.

"I'll bet he's going for his car," I whispered, holding Bottom's mouth as I heard gutteral noises begin in his throat. The night wind was fairly strong by now and the rustlings from the trees were enough to cover our little sounds. "It's down the road past Caroline's house," I added, "unless he has moved it, and I don't think he could have had time."

"You stay here and keep watch," hissed Collie.

"I'm going to find the sheriff by the carriage house and bring him back here." He held my shoulders tightly a moment. "Don't move from this spot until I get back," he said firmly, climbing the wall.

And he was gone.

I watched Billy Ray's flashlight bob out past the church and then he was in the road and the light went out.

Bottom squirmed but I held his collar firmly, whispering to him until he calmed down and lay quietly beside me. All around us the insects tried to out-sing the wind in the elms, and any other time I could have enjoyed sitting beside the old wall listening to their antiphonal concert. But tonight each note sounded like the snapping of a twig beneath a foot or the rustling of leaves as someone tried to slip up behind me.

Why was Collie taking so long?

Bottom mumbled a protest and tried to stand. And then his protest became a snarl as rough hands grabbed my head, muffling my mouth and jerking me rudely backward with my back held firmly against the rough brick of the wall.

Billy Ray Johnson whispered fiercely into my ear. "Shut that dog up or I'll shoot him and you right here." And he waved a gun with what I supposed to be a silencer on it in my face. "Do it quietly," he ordered, loosening his hold on my mouth enough for me to speak to Bottom.

"Send him to the house," he told me when I had the dog under control.

I knew the preacher didn't like Bottom, and I was afraid he would shoot him if he left my side, but I was also afraid he would shoot him anyway if I didn't obey.

So I said, "Go to the house, Bottom." And then I added the word that saved his life: "Run!"

This was the dog's signal to run in circles at great speed, his main way of getting exercise in the small yard we had in the city. Thinking we were about to play, he leaped the wall and started racing around in circles among the elm trees. Billy Ray took aim and fired a couple of shots at him as he dashed out into the open lawn and became silhouetted against the lighted windows of the house. Somehow Bottom sensed this was no game and disappeared toward the back yard.

Billy Ray swore under his breath and climbed over the wall without too much difficulty. He had his cane hooked over his left arm with which he was holding me and it bumped against me as he pushed and pulled me across the yard to the cemetery. I strained, looking back over my shoulder to see if Collie and the sheriff might be coming.

He laughed. "Don't be looking for the professor," he said. "I called the sheriff before he could.

Why that sheriff has been a member of my church for eight years. He'd believe anything I told him and I told him plenty."

We reached the graveyard fence and he pushed open the pillar.

I pulled my mouth away from his hand. "But you have no proof to show him," I protested.

"Well," he drawled, "I have those two rolls of film."

"What good could they do?"

"Those pictures show this trap door from every angle, closed and open and was I surprised that they were using my churchyard as a hiding place." His tone of voice was sickening. The fact I had had no supper didn't help the state of my stomach either.

"Climb in," he said, pushing me toward the ladder.

"Did you think I didn't know you were in here a while ago?"

"How did you know?" I asked, watching him maneuver down the ladder behind me. And wishing I had the strength to do something about him.

"I could smell you," he laughed.

"Smell me?"

"Certainly," he said keeping the gun pointed at me. "You have a faint sweet smell about you—your perfume, I guess—and also you brought in freshness with you."

"Why didn't you grab me then if you knew I was here?" I asked.

"My dear," he smiled sweetly as he talked, "I had to stall until Andrews had time to find you so that after the sheriff comes, I can lay the blame for your disappearance as well as David's at the professor's feet."

I glanced over at the cot and saw that the blankets were moving steadily with David's breathing. Now what? How could I with a broken arm do anything about freeing either of us.

"And besides," he continued, "I was busy moving the stuff down here." I looked over at the shelf where I had seen him place the boxes. There were many of them standing open with excelsior spilling out over the tops and into the dust. "Oh, yes," he said, "it isn't there now."

"What kind of stuff is it?" I asked, but my feigned ignorance didn't fool him.

"Don't give me that innocent stare, Brown Eyes," he sneered. "I know somehow your brother got the message across to you." He hooked his cane on the ladder.

Shifting his gun to the other hand, he gently stroked my hair, but the eyes that met mine were cold and hard.

I shook my head loose and stepped back from him. "What I don't understand," I said, eager to keep him talking, "is how you knew David had found you out and why he didn't go to the police."

He gave a sly laugh. "I saw him leave Goldengrove in a mad rush late Friday night and had a hunch he had heard or seen something he should-n't. Luckily for me the professor was away for the night so your brother couldn't give him the word. I simply followed him to town and one look at his face told me he knew so I just stayed with him and made him keep everything normal looking."

"But Collie saw him in the post office Saturday morning," I said puzzled.

"Ah, yes," he answered, "but he didn't see me standing out of sight with my trusty little friend here aimed at your brother." He grinned and patted the nasty-looking gun. "I was checking my box."

"But the call that night?"

"I slipped up there," he admitted. "He con-vinced me that if he didn't call you it might cause you to start checking up on him. But when I heard him talking in that cryptic way, I broke the connec-tion and put him down here where he could do me no harm. I guess I'll never know how he got that information to you."

I gave a short laugh hoping I sounded braver than I felt. "But the film?" I insisted, "When did he take those pictures?"

He frowned. "Last Wednesday when he was

nosing around he found the trapdoor but I came along and convinced him it was an old burial pit. I didn't know he had taken pictures of it."

I couldn't think of anything else to say at the moment.

Billy Ray was wearing same sort of hunting jacket with baggy pockets and old corduroy pants, still looking very much the part of the country gentleman.

Waving me toward the cot with his gun, he pulled some lengths of rope from one of his pockets.

"What now?" I asked trying to stall for time.

Time for what, I didn't know, but somehow I needed Collie to find us.

"I don't have time for any more conversation," he said rudely, and he motioned for me to sit down on the end of the cot beside David's feet. He knelt, stretching his lame leg out behind him, and first tied my left hand to a leg of the bed and then proceeded to tie my ankles together firmly.

Next he pulled a key from a pocket, uncovered David and unlocked his handcuffs, removing them and replacing them with a piece of rope. "Just in case somebody finds you sometime, it will look better if the handcuffs aren't there," he said grinning. "Metal won't burn; rope will."

I looked around in horror at the straw scattered thickly over the floor of the underground room and at the wooden shelves lining the walls, which were themselves shored up with pine boards. And I looked into the tunnel and saw the same type boards there. Could a fire started here spread all the way over to Goldengrove through this tunnel? Obviously there were air vents somewhere along the way. All I could hope was that there would not be enough air in the tunnel to keep the fire going very far.

"How could you do such a thing?" I asked, the horror sounding in my voice.

"Honey," he said, "for the amount of money I have stashed away in a little old bank in Birmingham, I could do almost anything." He laughed. "And I just about have."

From another pocket he took a tall candle, made a pile of straw near the ladder, then pushed the candle down in the straw until only a couple of inches stuck out.

I said, "I don't mean to sound trite but you won't get away with this." At the moment I was furious with him.

"Don't you worry about that," he said grimly, patting the thick bristly straw firmly around the base of the candle.

"It's a shame all the women Andrews drags in have to have scruples. This makes two I've had to dispose of." Then he took my purse from the floor where it had fallen, rummaged around in it and pulled out my scarf. He tied it securely over my mouth. "So you can't scream while I have the door open," he said and leaned down and kissed my forehead.

The man is unbalanced as well as mean, I thought to myself, and hoped he would forget that under my sling there were tips of fingers sticking out of my cast.

He flipped on a cigarette lighter and put fire to the candle. Then he hooked the cane over his arm and started up the ladder. "Oh, by the way," he said in parting, "I told the sheriff that your dog is mean and vicious and suggested he shoot him on sight, so don't expect old Bottom to rescue you."

With a grunt, he pushed the pillar closed, and the Reverend Mr. Billy Ray Johnson was gone.

I was alone with my poor drugged brother snoring beside me. But Brother Johnson had not finished. In a couple of minutes the dim light in our tomb went out and I was left watching that candle burn steadily toward all that straw.

And now at a time when it would be logical for me to weep, I sat dry-eyed, too furious to cry. I managed to work my broken arm loose from the sling which was not in itself an easy thing to do since the cloth cupped my elbow securely. Then I pulled the scarf off my mouth.

I reached over and pushed at David's legs. I needed to wake him up. He at least had one free hand. I yelled his name and beat on him with my cast until my arm was aching and my throat hoarse, but finally I saw the blankets stirring and heard him moaning.

"David, you must wake up," I pleaded.

"Can't," he muttered.

"You can!" I insisted. By straining toward him as far as possible, I could just reach his chin with the cast. I moved his head from side to side, pushing against it as firmly as I dared. I certainly didn't want to knock him out in my fervor to have him awake. He reached up with his free hand and flung my poor broken arm aside, almost throwing me off my place on the end of the cot.

I decided it was useless to try any further to rouse him and almost wished I myself were asleep instead of sitting there watching Billy Ray's little candle burn steadily down toward the spikes of straw. It gave off more light than I would have thought in the musty darkness, but on top of everything else, it was scented and its perfume added insult to the injury of my already queasy stomach.

It was not a very thick candle and it was burning fast. I kept struggling to free my left hand but only succeeded in tearing the skin on my wrist.

Once I thought I heard the trap door rattle and

held my breath for fear Billy Ray was returning, but when the door didn't open I felt disappointed, for secretly I guess I was hoping that some of the religion he had been preaching all those years might have rubbed off on him and made him change his mind about killing David and me.

There seemed to be nothing I could do to put out the candle. I thought of trying to kick a shoe over at it but realized that unless I could hit the candle right on the flame I would only succeed in knocking it over and starting the fire sooner. And anyway the shoes were too firmly on my feet to come off with my ankles tied together. I thought of swinging my feet around and rolling David off onto the floor and then trying to work the cot over to a place where I might be able to reach the candle but again gave up that idea as being another sure way of starting the fire more quickly.

So, there I was, helpless.

I thought of all sorts of things as I sat hunched over on the end of that iron cot watching Billy Ray's tiny flame. Most of all, though, I seemed to think about Collie and to wish for his strong arms around me. I had always scoffed at people who said they had fallen in love at first sight, yet here I was realizing that I was deeply in love with a man I had known only three days. At the thought of never seeing him again, the tears finally came. Which made me mad again because my nose always runs when I cry and I had absolutely no way of blowing it with one hand tied down and the other arm broken.

A puff of air came into the room, making the flame dip and sway and the first piece of straw caught fire. As I watched that first yellowish straw burn, I thought of the sparklers that as children David and I lighted at Christmas-time and held in our hands at arms length, wincing as the tiny sparks flew back at us while the shining flames sputtered to nothing at the ends of the little metal spears.

That first piece of straw struggled to catch the flame but soon sputtered out to nothing, leaving only a faint glow as it curled away from the candle.

The room was so quiet that I could hear the soft crackle made by the next straw as it caught a lick from the flame. This one seemed to burn a very long time and glowed bright red as it fell away to be joined by the next and the next and the next until soon the candle was completely hidden by a mass of fire that licked out in all directions and spewed and chewed greedily. I listened to the sounds and felt the heat and smelled the smoke, savoring these vital signs that I was at that moment alive.

Something popped, sending one spark out even as far as my feet and another to the blanket over David. I put out the glowing scrap on the floor by lifting my feet into the air and beating at it with my shoes and then smashed the one on the bed with my cast. The others I couldn't reach began slowly building into new little patches of fire perched on top of the straw.

The bitter smoke was burning my nose and throat, and I clawed at my running eyes with the cast while David began coughing in his sleep.

Another burst hit my ankle and burned through my sock, and there was nothing left that I could do except yell, so I started yelling. I yelled David's name. I yelled Billy Ray Johnson's name. I yelled Bottom's name. I even yelled my own name a time or two, I think. But mostly I yelled Collie's name over and over until I was exhausted.

When I paused for breath, I heard a high-pitched wailing far off and a dog barking. The wailing came closer and in my distress I imagined that the ghosts were coming to rescue David and me. All over much of the room streams of smoke were rising to the top and gathering there in a thick mass of churning blackness. I leaned over the edge of the cot on top of my bound hand and tried to put my head as near the floor as possible and then I realized the barking was close by.

Through the flames that had by now started up the ladder, I could see Bottom jumping and whining in the tunnel entry. He finally found a way around and raced over to me and David. Afraid that his fur would catch fire, I tried to yell at him now to go back, but every time I opened my mouth at this point, the smoke choked me. Yelping, Bottom leaped up on the cot and licked my face and lunged at David, jumping from one to the other of us up and down the little bed.

And then Collie plunged into our inferno from the tunnel, yelling my name as frantically as I had yelled his.

"Thank God, oh thank God!" he cried when he saw me alive and in one piece. He quickly found his pocketknife and cut me loose and then worked rapidly on David's bonds. My brother had begun to stir and cough more vigorously, but he still could not move himself around, so Collie shouted for me to go on through the tunnel and he took David by the shoulders and began dragging him across the room.

I grabbed my purse and paused to kick and push aside as much of the burning straw as I could to make a path for the others, and then we were all in the tunnel with Bottom running ahead, me shuffling along in the middle, and Collie, bent over with his hands under David's arms, running backwards as fast as he could go without hurting David.

It was a nightmare of darkness and smoke but in spite of that I was joyful to be out of the burning room with all of us alive. I stumbled over something and stopped to pick it up—a flashlight Collie had dropped on his way to us. What a good thing to have that beam of light dancing along ahead of us and behind us as I moved it along with us through our tunnel of escape.

And then all of a sudden Collie called to me to wait and I shined the light back while he closed some sort of door, and we were in a different sort of tunnel, this one shored up with brick instead of wood with even a floor of brick. The door was metal, a real fire door. It was hard to tell too much about anything because of the leftover smoke and I knew that we had to get out of there as soon as possible so we plunged on and finally the tunnel was curving upward and we came into a place obviously inside the house with a steep stairway snaking up beside a chimney.

I couldn't imagine how Collie would ever get David up those stairs, but I started up, shining the light behind me to show him the way. Bottom was already at the top of the stairway and behind him light was shining and there was no smoke.

We went through the closet into the black bedroom and then David was on the bed and Collie and I were falling into each other's arms with Bottom leaping up for his share of attention.

"We can't relax yet," said Collie pulling a blanket from a chest and throwing it over David's limp form. "I have to see if the sheriff needs help with

Billy Ray." He leaned over David to check his breathing and, satisfied that he looked all right, started to leave.

"Let me go with you," I urged as we heard Caroline coming up the back stairs so he asked her to see what she could do for David and to keep Bottom with her, and Collie and I sped downstairs and out the back door.

"You get behind a tree if trouble starts," he insisted as we ran hand-in-hand around the corner of the house.

"Surely the sheriff has him by now," I said, dodging a rose bush. "Please talk about tonight when you can."

Once again we were by the brick fence—the third time that night I had crouched in its shelter.

"Okay, we saw Billy Ray leave the cemetery and go off toward the road so the sheriff followed him and I went after you and knew where you had to be, but that brick pillar was jammed so I ran back to Marley's rooms and Bottom and I heard the ghosts in the bedroom closet so I kicked on the wall until a door opened. Do you believe in ghosts now, Anne?"

I just nodded because about then he motioned me to be quiet so we could listen. There seemed to be nothing to hear other than the night sounds, so Collie led me across the yard toward the carriage house where the sheriff's car was parked. As we reached the car, we heard someone walking up the lane from the road, so we hastened to hide behind the corner of the carriage house until we saw that it was the sheriff and that he was alone.

"I'm glad to see you're all right, young lady," he said. "I came to get my car."

"Where's the preacher?" asked Collie.

"He's at his house eating his supper and reading his newspaper," said the sheriff, "as if nothing has happened." He pushed back his uniform hat and scratched his head. "Are you absolutely sure he's got that heroin?"

"I'm positive he has it," I said. "I saw some empty boxes in that hole in the ground."

"Well," the sheriff answered, "I didn't get close enough for him to suspect I was there, but he went straight home. I eased around the house and watched him in the kitchen washing up and cooking his supper. If he's got any heroin there, he's not paying much attention to it."

"He didn't pick up a box somewhere around the church?" Collie asked.

"No, and he didn't go near his car," the sheriff answered.

"What I'm going to do now is drive over there and just talk to Brother Johnson. I have to find him in possession."

I was thinking back to those horrible minutes underground and I realized where the heroin was. "His hunting jacket!" I exclaimed. "Did you see him wearing a hunting jacket?"

The sheriff shook his head. "I wasn't close enough to tell what he was wearing until I looked through the kitchen window and he had on a pullover sweater in there." He climbed into his car and shut the door. And then he brightened up. "But there's a hunting jacket hanging on a nail on the back porch."

Collie said, "I'll bet the pockets of it are filled with heroin. We'll go with you over there." And he rushed me around the car and opened the door. When the car light came on and shone on our smutty faces, the sheriff asked what had happened to us. On the way over to the parsonage, Collie told him briefly about the fire and our narrow escape. And also that he would never build back that hole.

"Well," exclaimed the sheriff, "if I hadn't already been convinced that you were telling me the truth, Professor, that would do it."

As we turned into the parsonage driveway, Collie and I crouched down on the floor of the back seat and Collie said, "We'll go around back and let Anne look at that coat. If it's the one he was wearing earlier, we'll check the pockets and let you know."

"All right," replied the sheriff. "Meantime I'll keep that preacher busy out front."

"Be careful," I warned. "That man thinks he has killed David and me and he came right out and told me he was responsible for Marley's death."

Collie and the sheriff both made unpleasant comments under their breaths. Well to the side of the preacher's house, the sheriff stopped the car and went up to the front door. While we were waiting for him to go into the house, Collie whispered, "It was actually Bottom that convinced him I wasn't lying about Billy Ray. That good old dog came rushing up to us in the backyard while I was telling our story and the sheriff started to shoot him, saying Billy Ray had said he was vicious." He laughed softly. "And then Bottom sat down and offered the sheriff his paw to shake hands, so he knew that his own preacher had lied to him."

"Indeed that good old dog!" I exclaimed.

"Yes," he agreed, "and after that it was easy to convince him about everything else."

We heard the two men talking at the front door, and then the screen door slammed shut behind them as they went into the house. We slipped carefully out of the car and ran quietly around to the back porch where a dim light was burning and a hunting jacket was hanging on the wall. I nodded to Collie when we were close enough for me to recognize the coat as the one Billy Ray had been wearing earlier and Collie slipped out of his shoes and tiptoed across the porch to feel the bulging pockets. He reached in his hand and pulled out a pouch of something soft. The pockets were all stuffed with similar pouches. He took the coat from the hook on the wall and tried the back door. It was locked, so he came back to where I was waiting, put on his shoes and led me around the house to the front door.

"We'll just go up and ring the doorbell," he said, "and give this to the sheriff."

Billy Ray came to the door talking back over his shoulder to the sheriff, loudly asserting something about the professor. When he opened the door and saw Collie and me standing on his front porch, all the color drained from his face leaving rusty freckles and blue eyes bright against the white skin.

The sheriff moved in behind him and took his arm when Collie nodded and handed over the hunting jacket. He also opened the pouch in his hand and gave it to the sheriff who stuck in a finger and licked the substance he brought out. Billy Ray did not say a word as the sheriff led him out the door, and again I had the feeling of being set in the middle of a movie in slow motion as my fatigue and strain caught up with me.

The sheriff did some talking to Billy Ray, handcuffed him and put him in the front seat of his patrol car and Collie and I took our places again for a ride back to Goldengrove.

Still the preacher was silent. As we were getting out in the carport a few minutes later, I asked him where he had hidden David's car and he muttered something about some hidden space in the barn behind his garage.

And Billy Ray Johnson was off to jail for a long time.

Caroline met us at the back door with news from the hospital that Miss Allie was conscious and Doc Perkins was dead. Poor old Doc Perkins.

The news on David was good: Caroline had called her husband for help and between them they had given him a shower and found a pair of Collie's pajamas for him to wear, then put him to bed in a guest room after seeing he drank some soup and coffee. I vaguely remember her pouring some of the same soup down me and insisting I eat something that tasted warm and good.

And then Collie was kissing me and sending me off to take a hot bath and go to bed in my golden room. I don't even remember where Bottom slept. All I remember is that my sleep that night was as golden as the room around me and as peaceful as the golden elms whispering outside.

About the Author

Mary Beth Craft, a native of Mississippi, is retired and lives in New Orleans. She is the widow of Harvey M. Craft, the mother of four, the grand-mother of many, and the great-grandmother of several. *Goldengrove* is her first novel.